Con

LION'S DEN

F AR, FAR AWAY IN A small village just off the border of the Kalahari Desert there lived a little cat named Mia. Mia was a stray found in a sawmill, by a young boy who had by chance been playing near the boxes she'd taken as shelter. With no sign of a mother, he decided to take her to his grandmother, Nana, who was very good with little cats as she already had three of her own.

Nana was so excited about cute little Mia when she arrived. Mia, by the way, was the name given on account of how she would meow. Mia … Mia …

Now even though Nana was fond of little Mia, the other sister cats were much older and weren't used to their attention being shared with something so small. Nonetheless Mia had found a new family at the young age of seven weeks.

Time gradually moved on with the seasons changing to spring. Mia grew into a teenager and had fallen into the daily routine Nana had raised her to. Morning usually started with a fresh can of tuna – one bowl for each cat. The older sisters – Linky, Bella and Coco – had not changed over time and treated Mia as an outcast. Even around eating time, they pushed and shoved her aside.

"The young one eats last," Bella would say, and the others would laugh and follow her example.

After brunch Nana loved to sit out in her orchard and enjoy the breeze as the sun rose to its place in the sky. The girls would come and lie around her, wiping and cleaning themselves. Mia liked to use her outside time to run around and play – pouncing on anything that moved. Mia, as an outsider from a kitten, had become a bit of a tomcat. She was tough and didn't mind that she didn't fit in, as she always knew in her heart that there was a family of brothers and sisters – and even a mother – to which she belonged. Although Nana was her adopted mother whom she loved, Mia knew that one day she would find her real mother.

Around eleven o'clock every morning Nana had to go and do her daily errands, so the girls would be sent into the bedroom and locked in for safety as Nana couldn't bear the thought of losing one of her girls.

At this time the sisters would take their place on their favourite pillows and blankets and prepare for their afternoon nap. Nana would leave the television on for Mia as she knew Mia was restless and hoped it would calm her if there was something to watch.

So off she went, first giving each of them a little kiss on the head. Mia, ignoring the stares and hisses from the other sisters as they nodded off to sleep, made herself comfortable at the edge of the bed close to the television. Not trying to focus too much, she suddenly became interested in something on it. A type of cat family she'd never seen before. Her heart jumped with excitement as she pounced up to get a better look.

They were brown in colour – which Mia thought was similar to her orangey tinge. There were big ones and small ones but the most important thing was that they were a family who liked to play and pounce and protect one another. Something she'd never had but knew was real. Unable to keep her excitement in, she started running around the room from one end to the other.

"What's all this noise about, Mia?" Linky shouted.

"We're trying to nap here!" added Coco.

"My family! It's my family, I'm sure of it!" exclaimed Mia.

"Where? Where are they?" asked Bella, who now began to rise from her throne.

"On the TV! On the TV! I'm going to find them, and you'll be sorry for being so nasty to me. Then you'll see!"

The three sisters turned to the television and stared for a second before turning to each other and bursting into laughter.

"What's so funny?" demanded Mia.

"That's not your family," replied Bella.

"How could you possibly know?" Mia replied in disbelief, and the girls continued to giggle hysterically.

3

"Those are lions, silly! Jungle cats and house cats never mix, everyone knows that!" Linky replied.

"They are my family too! They play like me, they look similar to me and … and … I'm going to find them. I'll show all of you and then you can have your silly nap time in peace!"

At this, Coco tried to calm Mia. "Now, now, Mia, we're only trying …"

"Psssst! She's got a point." Bella interrupted quietly, winking at the other two.

"Hey, Mia, I happen to know where those lions are right now." Bella lured Mia to the window overlooking the horizon towards the open dry lands in the distance.

"Where, Bella? Tell me, please!"

Bella pointed to the far centre of a dry desert miles and miles outside of their little town. "There." Mia's eyes grew wide and her mind was racing with excitement. "I can even show you a way out of this house, but if I do, you have to leave before Nana gets back – or I may change my mind," Bella offered.

"Alright! Alright! I promise."

At this, Coco and Linky began to feel guilty. "No, Mia, I don't think this is a good idea. What about Nana?" said Linky.

Suddenly, Bella flipped the handle of the window and in came a gust of wind from the outside, like a silent voice calling Mia away. She became hypnotized by its sweet sound and jumped to the window. She struggled a little to get through the bars, but managed to squeeze her way out.

Her heart filled with sudden doubt, she looked back at what she was leaving – Coco and Linky looking nervous to the one side and Bella smirking mischievously to the other. Mia's pride kicked in. 'I'm going to find my family!' she thought to herself then darted up a tree and over the gate out into a whole new world. As she reached the small road that ran through the town …

BROOOOM!

A huge truck came racing past. Mia shrieked and her hair stood up on end, but she knew that this could be her only opportunity. She ran with all her might and hopped on the back. The ride was bumpy and rather noisy but it was heading in the direction of where she wanted to go and that was good enough for her. A smile came over her face while watching the town as the truck passed through. A familiar sight to the left – the factory where she'd been found as a kitten. "I knew it! I'm headed in the right direction, I'll be home in no time!" she shouted.

Suddenly a deep gruff voice echoed from a dark space in the back of the truck. "Who said that?" Mia's eyes opened wide with fear, as she'd never had contact with anyone outside of Nana's house before.

"Umm … it's me, Mia … the Lion."

Suddenly two gleamy blood-red eyes peered from the back. "Mia the Lion, hey?" the voice replied, "And what purpose would Mia the Lion have on the back of this here old truck?" The shady voice stood to its feet and hovered high above Mia. As her fear increased she began to stutter her words.

"I … g-going … t … t-to … the d … desert … t … to find my family."

The shady voice moved from the back and stepped into the light. A large bloodhound, old and wrinkled, stood before her, staring down. Suddenly he came to life.

"Road trip, hey? Why didn't you say so? Name's Hubert, Hubert the Hound. Mia the Lion – it's a pleasure to meet you. I tell you these rides can get so boring, it's an honour to have a lion as a guest. But say, aren't you a little small to be a lion?"

"Nope, they come in different sizes," she replied with confidence.

"Different sizes, hey? Well, I'm not one to judge. I always say every cat or, ehmm, every lion to his own. Welcome! So can I offer you some raw meat? You lions do like your raw meat?"

Although it was her first time she was liking the idea of being a

5

lion. It felt like she was somebody for a change – respected by others regardless of her size and age. Hubert dragged some of the raw meat over and Mia dove in.

"So, desert you say? Well, this here truck only goes up so far. Your best bet from there would be on foot. Where about is your family? 'Cause the desert's a pretty big place for one little lion to be wandering around."

Mia wondered to herself for a second, maybe she hadn't thought this out too well. Then suddenly she remembered what she had seen on the television.

"Oh, there's a big tree they usually sit around. I'm looking for that," she replied.

"Tree, hey? Well, I guess you lions would know better than me. I'm so old I can barely even see the door before I walk into it," Hubert replied, laughing at himself.

"Boy, am I full! That raw meat was sure good!" But not as good as the tuna she was used to at home, she thought.

"It was my pleasure. Maybe one day I'll come and visit you and your family and you can repay the favour."

"It's a deal!" Mia replied.

"Well, let's get some shut-eye, there's still a bit of a drive ahead of us and you are going to need all the rest you can get," Hubert suggested as he lay back down off his long legs. Mia found a place in a corner. Looking outwards, she watched the last few buildings of her little town as she fell to sleep …

"Rise and shine, sleepy head! We've reached home. Well, mine at least," Hubert shouted, unaware of how loud he was. He sent Mia into a panic as she woke up.

"Where? Where am I?!"

"You're on the border of the Kalahari Desert. Out there somewhere is a tree with your family. This here is my cabin I live in with my master. It ain't much but you're welcome to stay anytime."

Mia, lost in amazement, stared out into the desert. Its vastness was unreal – the colours fresh and bright, trees all over and grass as

6

tall as she'd ever seen. In the far distance the sun rising in the east never looked so proud. She took a deep breath and inhaled the fresh air.

"Thanks, Hubert the Hound, but I know where my home is for the first time."

"Well then, get out there, little miss, and find them," Hubert shouted out excitedly.

Mia ran up to Hubert and gave him a hug, then darted off into the desert, even more determined now than before. Full of energy, she didn't slow down for a second, looking out at every big tree around her. Slowly losing sight of the cabin, she journeyed deeper and deeper into the desert.

Unaware of the dangers that lay ahead Mia ventured without caution, finding it hard not to get distracted by the many bugs and butterflies, much like those she used to play with in the garden – only these were larger and more colourful. Jumping from one leap to the next, she found herself much at home.

But little did she know, another creature who found itself very much at home was hovering above. Watching her every move patiently … quietly.

It was a colony of vultures.

"Say, what do you think that village cat is doing all the way out here?" one said. The vultures' knowledge of animals in and around the desert was vast as they were always looking for new prey.

"I don't know but it's only a matter of time and it'll be ours for the taking," another giggled. "That herd of elephants ahead should do the stomping and we'll do the chomping, let's just lay back and watch."

Lower down, Mia found herself chasing a butterfly who had led her right in-between a herd of elephants. As a matter of fact, right into one of the elephant's legs.

"What's all this?!" the elephant yelled. "What are you trying to do?"

This caught the herd's attention and they gathered around. Mia, realising she had got herself into a bit of trouble, went into stutter mode again.

"B-B-B, C-C-C, MEOW."

"Well? What is it? Speak up!" the elephant continued. "What are you and what do you want?"

"W-well, I'm a-a lion, mister b … big grey thing," Mia quivered. Then she remembered her first experience with Hubert and that there was no reason to be afraid of anything bigger than herself. Her confidence grew as she dusted herself off.

"What did she say?" one elephant asked.

"Speak up!" said another.

"Um. Yes. I'm a lion and I'm looking for my family. Has anyone seen them?"

"SHE'S A LION!" came a frantic shriek from the back of the herd. The herd became hysterical while the leader stayed calm.

"Hold on! Hold on!" commanded Tantor, the general of the elephants.

"Hold on?" shouted another.

"When there's one there's usually two or three or four or five or …"

"OK, OK, we get the point, Phil," interrupted Tantor.

"I'm just saying," Phil murmured.

Tantor turned to Mia and started to observe her carefully. "You're rather small for a lion. Nevertheless, lions and elephants don't mix – it's a rule. You knowing this and still running in amongst us says you're either very brave or very, very stupid," he stated. "So which is it, little lion?"

"I only wish to find my family. I was lost but I need to find them so I can be a family like you are with yours. I mean you no harm," Mia answered.

"Ha! No harm until you grow up and then what?" Phil piped up again.

"Phil, can you shut up?" demanded Tantor. "As irritating as he may be, he is right – lions and elephants are enemies and to help you would no doubt be the wrong choice for our own, so my advice is to run along swiftly and think twice before charging amongst an elephant herd again. Understood?"

Mia turned away and continued with her tiring quest. Now sad, as she was reminded of her sisters back home in the village who would treat her the same. The fun had ended abruptly and for the first time she knew what it was like to be alone. Thoughts of her old Nana and the comforts of her pillow in her room were fresh on her mind. Not sure which way to go, the true size of the desert became a dawning reality.

Still flying above, the vultures stared in amazement.

"Why didn't they … you know?!" said one.

"I don't know – now get your breath out of my face! Let's go down for a closer look. If the cat thinks it's a lion then we'll give it a lion," replied the other. Down they went, surrounding a very sad and lost Mia.

"Hey, lion!" shrieked one of the vultures, while winking at his buddies.

Mia ignored this and continued to walk on.

"Hey, lion, word is you're looking for your family," he continued.

Mia now paid attention and her face lit up again.

"How did you know that? Can you help?"

"Yeah, yeah, sure, we see everything from the sky, as a matter of fact, there's a pride of them just beyond that stretch of grass."

Before even saying another word, Mia darted off faster than ever before, racing through the long grass. The vultures stayed back, laughing away for they had deceived her.

Suddenly the grass ended and the ground sloped down. It was too late for her to stop. She tumbled down the hill and knocked herself out. Her eyes began to open and close as she slipped in and out of consciousness. First she saw the vultures standing over her, and next they flew off frantically. A face appeared over her.

"You, you're like me!"

There before Mia stood a baby lion cub, who had scared the vultures away. She rose to her feet and smiled. The cub started to circle around her in amazement.

"Where are you from? Where's your pride?" asked the cub.

"Well, I'm from far away, I guess," Mia replied.

"Well, welcome. My name's Lusark."

"My name is Mia."

"Come on, Mia, there's so many you must meet over here."

Mia and the cub ran off over hills and in-between thorn trees to an area close to a waterhole. She stopped abruptly and stared in amazement, for there, on the other side, was a pride of lions all sitting together, bathing one another and drinking from the bank, just like she had seen on the television.

"Come on, what are you waiting for? I'll race you!" shouted Lusark excitedly.

Mia darted off, chasing after Lusark until they reached the pride.

"Lusark, where have you been?" his mother yelled from the pack.

"Hunting, and look what I found! Another lion!" he replied.

"Oh! Why, hello, what is your name, little one?" Lusark's mother asked.

"Mia is my name."

"Why, hello, little Mia," the mother greeted kindly. "I am Sansabi."

"Mother, she is my new best friend," declared Lusark.

"Oh well, OK," Sansabi replied with a slight giggle. "If you say so, Lusark. Mia, welcome, please join us for feeding time," the mother invited.

Mia nodded eagerly and ran into the pack where she was introduced to the pride.

Sansabi turned to her sister, who seemed confused, for they both knew Mia was no lion, but if she was to Lusark and the cubs then she was to the elders.

They enjoyed their late lunch, feeding and gathering around a large tree, preparing for the night, they all snuggled up to one another and began to fall asleep.

"Tomorrow we're going to have so much fun, Mia. All the men should be arriving back in the next day or two and then you can meet my father. Sleep tight," rambled Lusark.

"Can't wait, sleep tight!" replied Mia.

She took in the last bit of red light the sun gave off before it disappeared into the horizon. The view was amazing, and Mia was pleased. She couldn't believe how lucky she was to have found the lions. For the first time she had a mother to snuggle up to and a brother to protect her .Slowly she nodded off …

Morning came quickly in the desert, with clear blue skies and bright rays of sunlight. Mia was woken with a rather hard nudge from Lusark.

"Get up, sleepy head, it's time for our morning baths and then we prepare for the hunt of the day."

"Baths? Hunt? Hunt what?" replied Mia, appearing confused.

"Come, you'll see."

Mia followed Lusark down the hillside to a quiet spot near the waterhole, covered in luscious green grass. There they lay with the rest of the lionesses and their young, each cub being cleaned with the large tongues of the elders.

"Come, Mia, cleanliness comes first amongst us lions," said Sansabi in a firm motherly tone. Mia stepped up and was licked from one side to the next with one swift move from Sansabi.

"There we go," she said, "all done."

Mia, looking like a soaked porcupine, shook off to get dry.

"Wow! That would have taken me at least an hour, thanks."

"My pleasure, young lady, now on your way to the other cubs, we must plan the hunt to feed our hungry males when they arrive later today."

Mia ran off, now not only feeling like a lion but smelling like one too. More and more her reality set in.

But would Mia stand the true test of being a lion and have the stomach to kill another animal? Little did she know what was right around the corner.

"Hey, Lusark! What are you guys playing?" asked Mia. "Can I join?"

"Sure, we're practising the great hunt of the elephants," replied one of the cubs.

"Elephants?" Mia questioned. "Why the elephants?"

"Alright, cubs, gather up," Sansabi ordered. "You cubs follow swiftly behind and keep your distance, but watch our every move. There's a herd of elephants not far from here and we'll need to hurry if we want to finish before the men arrive back."

The cubs raced off to keep up as the lionesses shot into the distance.

"Why elephants? Wait, guys!"

"Hurry, no time to chat!" Lusark shouted back.

Mia's conscience played on her mind as she raced through the African desert after the lionesses. After she had already met the elephants and told them she wasn't there to attack them, how would it look? In a way she felt responsible for protecting them. Her morals lay at the very edge of her mind.

"Shhh," Sansabi said as she crouched and disappeared into a patch of long grass.

"What's going on?" asked Mia nervously.

"Shhh! We wait here silently. The elephants are just over that hill. If they hear us it'll spoil the surprise attack," Lusark explained.

"They are?" Mia squeaked. I can't let this happen, Mia thought as she peered over the hill, watching Sansabi and the other lionesses moving in on the pack. "I have to try to stop them, let me talk to Sansabi and see if I could change her mind," she said softly to herself. Mia darted up and across the field towards Sansabi.

"Mia, no!" shouted Lusark.

"Say, isn't that the lion, that small lion that ran into us the other day?" shouted one of the elephants.

Tantor turned to check.

"Why, you're spot on, and I told her never to come back …" he said.

"And she's running to a bigger lion!" shouted another frantically.

"I knew it!" Tantor yelled. "So she's trying to sneak up on us with her older friends, hey?" Tantor acted quickly. "Elephants! Charge!"

Suddenly the pack of lionesses was surrounded by stampeding elephants.

"Retreat, lions!" Sansabi ordered.

Mia suddenly realised the elephants weren't slowing down to thank her and found herself running for her life instead.

"And don't try it again!" Tantor screamed at the fleeing lions. "Those lions are all the same," he added to his herd.

The lions ran a far distance before stopping and regrouping.

Sansabi was furious. "Where is she?" she hissed. "Do you realise what you've done? We won't have anything for the males to eat when they arrive. The King will be furious."

"I-I was j-just trying to ..." Mia tried to explain.

"There is no excuse. So keep your words to yourself!"

Another lion shouted and ordered, "Everyone back home but keep your eyes open for more livestock."

The day moved slowly on the journey back to the great tree. Mia's words had disappeared from her mouth and on arrival she found herself sitting on her own.

"They're here!" shrieked a lioness, "and we have no food. Who will pay for this insult to the King?"

Sansabi stood up, "I will, it was my fault."

Suddenly the ground began to shake as the large males fed into the pack. The King came in aggressively, sniffing and looking between the lionesses, who now couldn't even look him in the eye.

"What is this?" the King demanded, "where is the food?"

"Sire, … we …," Sansabi started to explain.

"Choose your words carefully, Sansabi. Our hunger has no sense of humour."

"There is no excuse, Sire. I have failed you."

"What! And you think your brave honesty would redeem you." The King charged towards her until they were face to face. "We have travelled for days looking for new land for the pride and you honour our labours with such little respect? Well, an example shall be made of you, Sansabi. It shall indeed!" exclaimed the King, raising his paw to the air and stretching out his claws.

Mia was afraid but overwhelmed by guilt. "Wait! It was my fault. Blame me!" Mia shouted from behind.

"What? Who said that? Show yourself." The King moved in-between the pack. "I said show yourself."

"Here I am."

The King looked down at Mia. Suddenly he became frantic with laughter.

"You are to blame? Ha, ha, ha! That is the craziest, funniest thing I've heard all day!" Then in a heartbeat his face changed to one of anger. "Just what are you even doing here – village cat! You are not even a lion; I should eat you right where you stand!"

"But, father, she is a lion like me and she's my friend," cried Lusark.

"You, my son, will speak when spoken to!" He now addressed the whole pride. "Whatever has been going on here stops now; obviously this madness is slightly my fault. I haven't been strict enough with you. Come now, we leave for the highlands. Lionesses will track, hunt and serve twice as much food as was expected. And as for you, village cat – son, she is not even a lion. She is already full-grown and will never be like us. Go back to your village and consider my kind grace of not eating you a favour for my son. Lusark, let us go."

Lusark turned to Mia with disappointment. "You aren't really … a lion? Why did you lie to me?"

"I really thought I was. But your father is right. I guess I was just looking for a family of my own."

Lusark walked off with a tear in his eye, knowing that his friendship was no more and that he had to leave Mia.

Mia watched as the pride ran off into the distance. Sad and alone, she let go of her hope and decided to venture her days out in the desert by herself. Not caring where she went, she headed off. Through the night, back into the harsh day she travelled over the dry desert sand, passed the large Baobab trees and into the long grass. Having no knowledge of the desert, she became hungry and thirsty.

The day moved on into the afternoon and the distance travelled was uncertain. Mia was exhausted and couldn't move another muscle. She rested her head for a second but slipped into a deep sleep. She saw a picture of her grandmother serving tuna and holding her up to give her a little kiss on the head. Even the sisters seemed friendlier after being exposed to the desert. Instantly she felt most comfortable and happy. The pressure to be accepted was not so hard.

SLIRRRP …

Mia was woken with a giant lick to the face.

"Mia," a voice called. "It's me. Hubert. Wake up, little one."

"Hubert? How did I get here?"

"Barely, but you somehow stumbled out of the desert and right back to the cabin."

Looking up, a sense of relief came over her.

"I guess it's that lion sense of direction though. Did you manage to find your family?" asked old Hubert.

"I'm not a lion, Hubert. I'm a village cat, and will never be a lion," sobbed Mia.

"I kinda gathered that, but I guessed if you believed it then there was no reason for me not to."

"Well, I tried but the lions chased me away for scaring off the elephants. Then they left me behind and headed to the highlands."

The highlands? Why does that sound familiar? Hubert thought to himself.

"Hmmm, wait a minute, there were hunters buying guns from my master a day or two ago. They were headed for the highlands."

"Oh no! I have to warn the lions!" cried Mia.

"You'll never be able to make it in time," Hubert responded.

"I may not be a lion, but I wasn't an elephant either. I have to help them. Thanks, Hubert."

She took a sip of water and then raced back into the desert. Not stopping for a rest. Into the cold desert night. Hoping she was not too late. Not even being tired was going to stop her though. Their lives rested on her warning them.

Not far west of her though was a group of hunters looking for a prize trophy to take back. The trophy was the King of the Jungle himself. The scout they had hired spoke of large lion footprints that he'd seen inside a valley just behind the high grounds. Down a rocky slope they went, deeper and deeper towards the waterhole. It was a beautiful oasis of trees and water and was the exact place the King had planned on moving the pride.

"Turn the vehicle off. We'll camp out here and wait for the right moment," said one of the hunters, whose name was William.

"Sounds good, I'll get the guns loaded!" shouted the other, whose name was Eliot.

"Keep your voice down, don't you forget that lions have ears and if they hear you they, they ... Oh never mind, just shut up!" ordered William.

"Loaded the guns," whispered Eliot.

"Right, well it's late, let's get some shut-eye. The waterhole will definitely be surrounded by thirsty lions come morning," suggested William as he made himself comfortable in the front seat.

The desert was covered in a black sheet of sky. The stars looked like sparkling diamonds. Not far from the hunters the lions were preparing for their rest too, just off from the valley on top of the high grounds.

The King spoke up. "Uhmm! Well, I guess we've had some setbacks recently but that's all about to change. Tomorrow, my fellow lions, we settle into our new home. Down the highland slopes and into the valley you will find plenty of food and water to fill our bellies. Morning dawns, time to rest."

All the lions and the hunters had slipped into a peaceful sleep while the moon watched over them.

One little creature was still awake. Mia used the moon for light and persevered on through the night to save the lions from the hunters. Over rocks and through trees, facing the chilling noises of the desert night. She had reached the high grounds.

The sun had just started to rise and the lions were preparing to move.

"Right, all together now," Sansabi directed the cubs.

"Mum, I miss Mia."

"I know, Lusark, but you know she'll never be one of us."

"Could the King have been wrong? I mean she looked similar to me."

"One day you will understand. Now come, little one, our journey is nearing its end."

Lusark straggled behind as the pride moved on away from the sunrise. Heartbroken, he feared he'd never see his friend again. Looking back one more time, his eyes opened wide in disbelief. The sun was shining bright so it was hard for him to see.

"MIA," he heard, as Mia gave one last meow to catch the pride's attention. Drained and tired, she crawled up to the patch where Lusark stood.

"Mia! It's you. How did you find us? I'm so glad you are back."

All the cubs ran back to greet her. But this was not a good thing for the King. He stormed through the pack and braked hard in front of her.

"You have returned against my wishes and have ignored my kindness. Have you any last words, village cat?" the King roared!

"I came to warn you. Hunters wait for you in these hills."

17

"Ha! You spend a few days in the desert and you think you know all. I've checked these paths and the valley. There are no hunters and if there were my fleet and I would have spotted them."

"A friend has seen them buying guns and heard them speaking of lions in the high grounds," Mia tried to explain.

The King looked unsure. But pride soon took over.

Sansabi out of concern tried to convince him. "Shouldn't we listen to her, Your Highness?"

"Nonsense! All nonsense! To get herself back in the pride. Why, so you can chase more livestock away? So we can starve to death! Pride, move on!"

"But …," Sansabi tried again but was interrupted.

"But nothing!" the King groaned. "I have spent too much time finding this new home to have it spoilt or postponed any further. Now move, Sansabi."

This time the whole pride moved on, uncertain of the King's judgement. But still they must listen. Those who disagree must be strong enough to challenge the strength of the King.

"As for you, little Mia, this is your last chance." The King turned off and raced to the head of the pack.

Mia started to move back. "You are making a mistake." Remembering how she had to save the elephants on her own, she darted to the side and raced further along the high grounds to get a better view of the valley. Looking for something out of the ordinary that would give the hunters' position away.

"There it is." She spotted a reflection of light from one of the hunter's scopes on the other side of the bay. Down she went, unsure of what she would do when she got there.

"I see them, eight, nine, ten of them and little ones too. Which one first, William? Which one?"

"Patience, Eliot. Let them get lower down and more into the open. Perhaps when they are drinking water?"

The hunters waited silently as the lions arrived.

18

"See how beautiful." The King presented their new home to the pride, who shared the excitement as they arrived.

"And no hunters as that village cat had said. I know this desert like the back of my paw. Look, plenty of water to drink as you please."

The King ran up to take the first sip.

"Easy does it, we've got the big one in sight," William whispered from the other side of the waterhole. "I'm taking the first shot."

Suddenly Mia jumped onto the back of the truck and squeaked out the loudest meow she had ever meowed before.

MEOW!

The hunters caught a fright and turned around slowly.

Phil squeaked, "A lion?"

"Ha, ha, ha, ha. I don't know what you are doing out here, little pussy cat, but you're a long way from home."

William reached out for Mia. "Come here, little kitty."

Mia dove at William, scratching his face while hissing at Eliot.

"Ahhhhh, it's scratching me, help me, Eliot."

BANG!

William's gun went off by mistake, loud and clear for the lions to hear. Eliot in anger grabbed Mia off and held her up by the back of her neck. The pride on the other side were already frantic!

"Quick, Sansabi, take the cubs to shelter. Men over there across the waters. Let's split up and regroup around that truck for a little appetiser," the King ordered.

"One of them has got the cat, Sire."

The King thought to himself, she was right. "Let's move," he shouted.

Across the river Eliot, who was holding Mia, turned to see if the lions had heard the shot. But he saw no lions.

"Why you little … Chasing away the lions to save them, hey? Quite clever for a pussy cat but now who's going to save you? Lions and kitties never mix. Do you think they care about you one stinking bit? Pass her to me, Eliot."

"Ahhh, William."

"Just hand her over. I'm going to make an example of an animal when it tries to stop me."

"I think if you could turn around, Will, you'll know what I wanted to tell you."

"Oh, what is it? Yieks! B-b-b lions. BIG ONES!"

The King and his men slowly moved in on the hunters. He jumped on the front of the truck and gave out a mighty roar. ROAARRR! And stared straight into William's eyes.

"Is this your little pussy cat? I didn't know. I mean how could I have known …? I'm just going to put her down. There," he laughed, but only out of fear.

Mia looked proud to have such intimidating friends.

William started to cry. "Eliot, they're going to eat us, aren't they? We'll just get in the truck slowly, they haven't done anything yet."

"I'm with you, Will. Nice lions, I'm just going to take my gun and leave …"

The King growled at Eliot.

"N-n-n-n-no, no, no, I'm not taking the gun, y-y-y-y-you can have it, Mr Lion."

"Eliot, just get in, start the engine slowly and move out even slower."

"I'm trying. I'm too nervous, OK?"

The lions moved to the side of the vehicle with Mia standing in front. Eliot looked across and gave them an awkward smile.

"Drive already, you idiot," William yelled.

"OK, OK."

Eliot put the truck in gear and accelerated. But instead of going backwards up the rocky slope they dove forwards into the waterhole. Mia and the lions started to laugh as the truck drifted away downstream.

"Wrong gear perhaps, El?"

"I told you I was nervous."

William started crying again.

"Well, Will, at least we got away."

"Yes, yes we did. Did you also know, El, that Africa's waters are infested with crocodiles?"

At that moment one popped its head up in the distance. The hunter's screams were heard as they floated away.

With little time to talk, Mia and the men gathered back by the females and the cubs.

"Mia, you saved us," shouted the lions. "Hooray!"

All came to stand around her to give her their thanks and appreciation, but one stood back without a word being said. The pride came to silence to respect the King's words. Mia, uncertain where she stood with the King, approached him and bowed her head. His head was held high to his pride. He looked down for a second then smiled. Took a deep breath and placed his paw on her shoulder.

"You have the spirit of the lion and, covered in sand like you are, you even look like one. I was mistaken and I invite you openly to join the pride."

Life came to the pride as they all celebrated the great news.

"Hold on, hold on. She has something to say," the King interrupted.

"My whole life I thought I have been without a family. It's why I came out here looking for this. We seemed similar in many different ways, and although I now know I may never find my true family that family is everywhere you go. Whether you are the same or not. And it's the efforts you make that keep the family strong. You are my family, but there is an old lady back in the village that put effort into my happiness every day and it's time for me to go back and give that to her."

Sansabi stepped up to Mia, "A noble choice, Mia. There is much we could learn from such a being. Know that you are always welcome here amongst the lions."

Mia said her goodbyes and left for her journey back to the village where she truly belonged. After all, she hadn't had tuna in days.

What happened there? Well, that's another story.

THE TIGERS
OF BASTET

I T WAS A COLD, COLD winter's day in the little village Mia had finally settled down in and called home. As a matter of fact, it had been one of the coldest winters the village had ever seen.

All was covered with snow, from the trees to the streets and even the roofs of every house. With not a person in sight the chilling noise of the wind could be heard as it froze everything in its path. Tucked in and unaware of the village's cold complexion was Mia, lying close to the warm fireplace on a new pillow that Nana had bought her. It was a surprise gift as she was so happy that Mia had found her way home. Nana hadn't been sure where Mia had disappeared to, but was convinced it was a filthy place when she saw the amount of dirt and sand she was covered in.

Mia lay still in a deep sleep, curled up in a ball. Next to her were her three sisters, Coco, Bella and Linky. They had decided that Mia wasn't so bad after all and had made their peace with her. Besides, if they didn't they wouldn't have been allowed to lie on Mia's new pillow. Nana sat close by on her old rocking chair that creaked more than it rocked, knitting jerseys for the long winter ahead.

Suddenly there was a loud, hurried knock at the door. Mia and the sisters jumped up in shock.

Nana was concerned. "Who could possibly be knocking at the door in this weather?"

"Hello, is anyone there? I'm from the post office, doing a delivery," said a voice. "It's as cold as a fridge out here, is anyone there? The faster you answer the faster I get back to heating up my behind."

Nana raced to the door. "Oh yes, yes, terribly sorry. Do come in. Delivery, you say? Well, I can't think of anyone who would send me something."

"It's a letter, and by the looks of the postage stamp it's from India," replied the postman.

24

"India? But I don't know anyone from India," Nana said, sounding confused.

"OK, well I'm just here to deliver it, Ma'am, and it's really cold and I have plenty more deliveries, so if you could just sign here I'll be on my way."

"Certainly," she replied, while signing the delivery sheet.

The postman passed a thin package from his bag and then raced off towards his van. "Have a nice day!" he yelled as he drove away.

Mia and the sisters sat watching from the fireplace with wide eyes. Who was this strange man and what did he want with their Nana?

"What's India?" Mia asked the sisters.

"Oh, that's easy, Mia, India is a spice for cooking food, Nana uses it all the time," said Coco, who was looking rather impressed with herself over her vast knowledge of cuisine and spices. Bella and Linky laughed.

"Sometimes I wonder if we're even related, Coco," said Bella.

"India is a country on the other side of the planet where people and animals live, just like us here in Africa," replied Linky.

"Well, Linky, it's not just normal animals like us that live there," said Bella.

"It's also where the king of all the cats lives. The largest and fiercest of them all. IT'S THE TIGER!" Bella shouted out, trying to give the girls a fright.

"The tiger? Wow!" replied Mia, whose eyes were so big from excitement they almost popped out of her head.

"They say a tiger is so big that when it walks the ground shakes, when it roars you have to cover your ears or you'll go deaf from the noise. And anyone who crosses its path will never live to tell the tale."

Bella had Mia mesmerized with the story so much, that she had forgotten how to speak. "Wow," she said, and continued to drift off into her imagination.

At this point Nana had found her way back to her rocking chair where she had begun to open the letter. Reading out loud, she tried to make sense of it.

> "Dear Rosemary," (which was of course Nana's real name)
>
> "It's been two years too long since we have last seen each other. I've been stuck in India long enough to call it home. Research on the jungle animals' strange behaviour has led me to many dead ends and has me needing a short break.
>
> Inside the envelope is a ticket to come and visit me in India. I have a lovely place you can stay at. Besides, it'll give us a chance to catch up and take you out of that cold climate you're stuck in. Please do consider. Look forward to hearing from you and seeing you even sooner.
>
> Your old friend,
> Edith"

Nana paused for a quick second, then jumped out of her squeaky old chair in a frenzy of excitement. "I'm going to India!" she shouted. "No more blankets and firewood! No more runny noses and certainly no more …" Suddenly her attention moved to the four little heads sitting up, side by side, staring at her. "Oh no, but what about my girls? I could never leave you behind and there's no one I would trust to take care of you."

Mia and the girls looked too adorable to leave. "I know," she exclaimed. "I'll just have to take you girls with me. It's about time you finally got out of the house and where better than India. Girls, pack your things," she yelled as she raced into the bedroom.

"What things is she talking about?" asked Coco.

"Wow," said Mia, "I'll get to see a tiger."

"Mia, don't bet on it. And if you do I would advise you to run in the opposite direction," said Bella.

"Sorry, but did you guys just miss what Nana said? We're going to India!" shouted Linky.

The girls were excited and sat thinking of what they would see when they arrived in India. But they had no idea how they would get there and where 'there' even was. Nana packed through the night while the girls tried to sleep. The excitement was too much for them to handle.

Morning had dawned with another loud knock at the door, sending the cats into a frenzy.

"Airport t-t-t-transport, brrr," shouted a voice. The temperature had dropped another two degrees during the night, turning almost everything to ice.

"Coming! Be right there." Nana raced to the front with her baggage in hand. The girls still weren't sure what was to happen next but they were excited about the trip. She opened the door and let the driver in. He collected the bags, packed them in the shuttle, and returned with four plastic containers with a small steel grill in the front of each.

"Are you sure they'll be alright? Those girls are my angels and I'd never be able to live with myself if anything happened to them."

"Ma'am, we do this all the time, and I promise they'll be fine when you get to the other side," assured the driver. "They get a sleeping tablet before getting on the plane and sleep the whole way. They won't even know what's happening. In fact, if I could travel like that I would."

"Well, OK, if you say so," replied Nana, still weary.

"Wait. What are they talking about? Tablet, what tablet? And why is he bringing those cages here?" Mia squeaked anxiously. Each cat was put into one, from Coco to Linky to Bella.

"Mia, from here God only knows what comes next," Bella replied as she was stuffed into her cage. Finally, it was Mia's turn. But fighter as she was, she wasn't going without having something to say.

Meow! She screamed, hissed, scratched, clawed and even raised the hair on her back, but none was enough to stop her from going in.

"A little fighter, hey? We may have to increase your dose when we get to the airport. Just for your own safety."

So off they went, all caged up in the back of the shuttle to the airport. Mia was not pleased and neither were the other girls, but at that point all they could do was sit back and try to relax.

After a short drive the shuttle came to a standstill. The back doors were flung open and Nana had to say her goodbyes until after the flight when they would meet again. Then she walked away.

"I knew it. Nana's leaving us," said Coco.

"Just keep quiet and wait," replied Bella.

A strange man walked up to them and picked the cages up. Placed them on a trolley and whisked them away.

"You see, I'm always right," said Bella.

They arrived at a room of some sort where they received a serving of tuna.

"Ah, lovely first class treatment I'd have to say," Bella continued. She took a bite and then continued to ramble on … only this time in slow motion. "Eve … ry … thing is go … ing to be a … l … right." Then she dropped her head and fell into a deep sleep.

The others had already fallen asleep from the sleeping tablet that had been placed in the tuna. This was purely for their safety so they could sleep through the flight to India. Mia had received an extra strong dose just in case she woke up too soon. The cages were placed on the plane, Nana had found her seat and off to India they went.

Mia dreamt of the African jungle in all its glory. She saw the lions that had accepted her into their pride and the many wonderful butterflies and bugs she'd chased during her time spent there. She lay fast asleep as the plane crossed the Indian Ocean and into New Delhi, where it would land.

The journey was smooth and the girls were still fast asleep when Nana took her first steps off the plane. It was the first time she had seen India and was taken back by its beauty. The first thing she noticed though was how warm it was. The air was moist and the sun had given life back to her skin that the cold winter had taken.

The fresh scent of incense and spices drifted through the air. It was a welcoming smell that put a smile on her face. She took a deep breath.

"Good afternoon, Ma'am, my name is Papun. I will be guiding you to your luggage's destination and then from there if you will be needing a cab I will be showing you to one."

The people of India were a friendly, accommodating race and although English was not their strongest language they still tried. Flustered with all the attention and just how warmly she had been welcomed, Nana followed Papun and had almost forgotten her cats.

"Oh," she said. "What about my cats?"

"Don't worry, they will be brought to you in front when they are taken off the plane," Papun assured Nana as he led her into the airport.

Still on the plane were the girls in their cages. Bella, Linky and Coco had started to wake up and were not impressed that they were still locked in. Mia remained fast asleep from the extra dose they had given her.

Suddenly a door opened and in came gushing bright beams of sunlight. Two men stood before the cages.

"Alright, I'll offload these little ones," said one of them. He proceeded by picking up the cages one by one and placing them on the back of a luggage carrier.

"I've never seen humans that looked like that," said Bella as she was placed on the baggage carrier.

"Me neither," replied Linky.

"I have," furthered Coco. This was followed by a very sarcastic look from the other two.

"Wait a minute. Where's Mia?" said Linky.

The baggage carrier had left before the loader could put all the cages on.

"Wait!" the loader yelled. "You forgot one of the cages. Ai ya yai! I am going to be in so much trouble."

At that moment another baggage carrier had passed the plane.

The loader, using the few cents he had for a brain, raced to put it on the back. Thinking, or maybe just hoping, that the cage would find its way back with the others. Little did he know this particular carrier was heading straight out of the airport to be serviced. Mia was still asleep. It appeared her flying experience was not so first class after all …

As soon as the carrier left the gates of the airport it picked up speed. But with all the potholes the ride became a rough one.

BANG!

"Another pothole!" the driver shouted as he looked in the rear-view mirror to check if everything was fine, then continued to look forward. Why had he not stopped when he saw the cage on the back?

Simple … the cage was no longer there …

"I'm really, really sorry about this, Ma'am. This has never happened before in all the days I have worked here." Papun had to explain to Nana why there were only three cages and three cats. "I'm sure it is around here somewhere and we will find it, I am definitely kind of certain about it."

Nana, lost for words, sat on a chair praying that nothing had happened to her beloved Mia.

"I say, the colour's not flattering but I can definitely do something with this steel grid," said a monkey as he commented on the cage. His name was Prince, a name he gave himself after listening in on a group of Englishmen taking a hike through India one day.

"Yes, a fine grid indeed," said another, whose name was Shootit. A name given to him by the same Englishmen just before they put him through some intense ducking and diving exercises as an initiation … or what he thought was an initiation … "Ah, and it brings out the colour in your eyes," Shootit continued while Prince posed. "Oh, what is that?"

"What is what?" replied Prince with a rather concerned look on his face.

"That! What is that disgusting fur ball inside of your new grid?"

Prince turned his attention to the inside of the cage. "NOOOOO!" he cried. "It's ruined. Quick, help me get it off."

"Not a chance. That is going to stain. And it is not coming near my coat!"

At that moment Mia started to wake up from all the commotion. Everything was still slightly blurry but slowly came into focus. She stepped out of the cage like everything was fine, took a huge stretch and yawned.

"Let's see, where's my tuna?" Suddenly it dawned on her. Trees, bushes, grass, fruit everywhere ...

"Ha, ha, ha!"

She turned around in disbelief, and then turned back again, hoping it had all gone.   "WHERE AM I?" she shouted.

"I say," said Prince.

"I do say," answered Shootit.

"Would you mind not shouting so loud? We have very sensitive ears. And would you mind stepping away from my grid, you're ruining it," requested Prince.

"Yes, get away. You're ruining his grid," said Shootit.

"I thought I was going to India," said Mia, who was still very shocked.

"This is India, silly thing," said Shootit.

Prince started to walk around and analyze Mia. "I say, what are you? Some sort of rodent?"

"Yes, what are you?" followed Shootit. "Some sort of rodent?"

"I'm a cat, if you don't mind," Mia replied, insulted.

"You're rather small to be a tiger, wouldn't you say?" asked Shootit.

"No, she's no tiger. I've seen these types before. It's a carry-around accessory. Everyone's got one nowadays," whispered Prince.

"Ahh," replied Shootit.

Prince walked up to Mia and picked her up, holding her in his armpit, back to front. "How do I look?"

"I'd have to say rather posh. This is a real head-turner, Prince.

31

Oh, do let me try."

Mia, still shocked, snapped out of it and pushed herself off Prince. "No, you may not try. Wait a minute. If this is India then where is everyone? Why am I here? And while I'm at it, what on earth are you two?" Prince and Shootit looked shocked.

"I say, she's a tiger accessory," explained Prince. "A small baby version so you can carry it around. Those other ones are just too big to lug around. But this, this is so convenient."

"Genius, Prince. That's you," said Shootit. "Genius!"

Mia's jaw dropped in amazement. She couldn't believe how dumb these two strange characters were. "Never mind, I'll sort this out by myself." She turned away and started heading through the jungle.

"Wait, if you go that way you'll go straight in-between the turf wars. And I'd hate to see such a lovely accessory get ruined," shouted Prince.

"Yes, hate it," continued Shootit.

"What's a turf war?" asked Mia.

"Oh, everyone knows the turf wars," said Shootit.

"You know the elephant gangs, the bear gangs, the monkey gangs," explained Prince.

"Which we don't conform to," followed Shootit.

"No, definitely not," replied Prince.

"GANGS?" answered Mia with wide eyes.

"Everyone's fighting for the jungle. Hell, even the birds have had a shot at it," replied Prince.

"And the tigers? Surely they have a part in it too?" Mia asked, but more for her own personal interest.

"HA, HA, HA," the monkeys laughed so hard they started rolling on the floor.

"What's so funny?"

"The tigers couldn't harm a fly. They're too busy sitting up in some temple, meditating," Prince explained while he continued to laugh.

"I thought they were the most feared animals in the jungle?"

"Yeah! If you're an ant!" answered Shootit, laughing.

"That's just a legend, it's not true," followed Prince.

"I know I should be finding my way out of here, but if I'm in the Indian jungle then I think it would be silly not to see the tigers. How would I get to the temple? I would love to see them," asked Mia.

"No, no, you don't want to do that. That means you'd have to go through the gangs," said Shootit.

"Well then, that's exactly what I'm going to do." Mia walked off into the depths of the jungle in search of the tigers. She herself couldn't be sure if those crazy monkeys had told her the truth.

"Oh, she's bluffing. No one's that stupid," whispered Prince.

"Well, looks like she's going, Prince."

"Oh, trotters. Oh, fuzz ball, if you must be a pest, then I suppose we could come with you for your safety. It's not every day a luscious accessory such as yourself comes along. Do wait for us!" shouted Prince.

So together they went. Prince, Shootit and their new tiger-coated carry-along accessory. Deeper and deeper they walked into the dense Indian jungle. Mia was amazed at how different it was to the African one she had spent time in, looking for the pride of lions. The trees grew tall to the sky. With so many they blocked the sun that could be seen for miles in Africa. Laced with millions of different greens, the jungle here looked fresh and new. Flowers in pinks and purples sprung out everywhere. Bees were busy collecting pollen while worms and bugs burrowed the soil. If the African jungle was the countryside this would have been the city.

Mia was again beside herself with the beauty that surrounded her. She was so distracted she'd even forgotten the fact that she was lost.

Not too far from there though, Nana had received the sad news that they could not find Mia anywhere in the airport. Not even her cage.

"It is possible that someone has stolen her," said Papun. "I am truly sorry. We will keep looking, but for now it's best you settle in with your friend."

Nana and the girls were devastated but knew finding her was out of their hands. She grabbed her things and left for Edith.

Back in the jungle Mia had some of her own problems to deal with. Those crazy monkeys had not given up on their crazy behaviour.

"Oh, please let me hold you. Just for a second," said Shootit.

"NO! I'm not a handbag or whatever it is you think I am," she explained.

"You let Prince carry you," he argued. "I just want to see if tiger suits my colour."

"If I let you pick me up, will you drop it once and for all?" she said.

"Deal," he answered. Shootit picked Mia up and started to pose like he was trying on a piece of clothing.

"Shootit, I swear sometimes I have to question if you know anything about fashion. The head goes to the back," explained Prince.

Shootit spun her around and then started to pose all over again. Mia did not look pleased. "How do I look? Does it suit me or what? I could actually get used to this. It's comfortable yet daring."

Suddenly a tall, dark shadow loomed over them. They all turned around slowly. Shootit dropped Mia and grabbed hold of Prince for protection. He was afraid, because standing before them was a giant elephant.

"Do you know what you are standing on?" he asked ferociously.

"GRASS?" they all shrieked.

"NO! You are standing on the land of the great Ranji, the elephant king. Anyone who stands on the land of the great Ranji either has gifts for him or is here to challenge his great army of elephants for his land. So which is it?"

"She made us come here. We don't even like land," explained

Prince as he quivered in his pants.

"Yeah, land, I don't even use it. Nope, never," followed Shootit.

"And who is this 'she'?" demanded the elephant.

Mia had seen elephants before in Africa but never one as aggressive as this one. Still, she felt she knew how to deal with them.

"I am Mia. I do not want your land. I only wish to pass so I can go to see the tigers."

The elephant broke out into a laughter that echoed through the bones of Mia and the monkeys.

"Tigers? I should have known such pathetic creatures would be looking for the tigers. You're no threat to my king, but still you must display a gift to pass these lands," the elephant demanded.

"But I have nothing to give. Perhaps if you let me through I could find one to bring back," she suggested.

"Agreed. But know this. If you return without one you will be crushed into powder like the spice that fills these lands."

Mia proceeded with her two monkey friends close behind. In the background they could still hear the elephant laughing about the tigers.

"I don't know what you plan to give King Ranji, but we're not going to be around when you give it to him. My coat just wouldn't look good as powder," whispered Prince.

"Yeah, powder not good," followed Shootit. "We'll lead you to the tigers then we're gone. Just up that hill, we're close to the temple now. Move along swiftly."

"We don't want to run into another gang," shouted Prince.

"Just where do you think you're going?" shouted a gruff voice from a dark part of the jungle.

"Not again," whimpered Shootit. They all turned to look for the voice but could see no one. The shadow spoke again.

"Trespassing on private property is punishable by death," continued the voice.

"But we just spoke to an elephant that said we could pass if we returned with a gift for King Ranji," explained Mia.

"That was for the elephant king, but what about the bear king, Amul?" The voice stepped out of the shadow and into the light. There before them stood a great big grizzly bear. Not as big as the elephant but twice as scary.

"YIKES! A B-B-B … BEAR!" Prince shouted out uncontrollably.

"What's the big deal? He's not as big as an elephant," said Mia.

"No, they don't stomp you. They chomp you," replied Prince.

"That's right," said the bear, "so move along with your business, but when you return you better have a gift for the very unforgiving king of the jungle, Amul. Understood?"

"But," said Mia.

"No, no, no," interrupted Shootit. "No 'buts', we will have a gift," he concluded as they dragged her away.

"No one says no to a bear, Mia, you silly, strange creature," explained Prince.

"But we already have to get the elephant king a gift. How will we ever find another gift for the bear king?" Mia replied. "And why are there so many kings in one jungle?"

"Don't worry about that, just be thankful you're alive and move on," Shootit added. "Now come along, we're almost there."

The further they went into the jungle the darker it started to get. It got colder because not much sunlight could penetrate through the thick trees. It was also harder for them to move along as the trees had started to wrap around everything. It looked as if no animal had come through the area in years. The only sounds heard were the creepy squeaks and creaks coming from the bugs watching from a hidden distance. Why were the other animals unafraid of the tigers? Mia thought to herself while heading up the steep hill to the temple. Even their home seemed like the scariest place that no other dared to venture. So why?

"Alright, see there, just through those bushes is the temple, but this is as far as we go," said Prince.

"But I thought you weren't scared of the tigers?"

36

"We're not, but just in case they've changed we're not getting involved in giving another gift to another king," replied Prince.

"Just for once it would be nice if we were given gifts," furthered Shootit.

"We'll wait here overnight and if you're not back by morning we'll consider you as damaged goods," said Prince, who began to eat the wax from his ear. "Now run along."

"Well, I guess I'll see you later. Thank you for your help," answered Mia.

She turned and started to move slowly towards the bushes. Remembering what Bella had said, she wasn't sure who to believe. Her heart started to beat harder as images of the tigers started to play on her mind. The shaking ground, the mighty roar that would certainly make you deaf and a hunger for raw meat only a monster could compete with.

As the day neared its end the afternoon sun shone through Nana's bedroom window. She sat near the phone, waiting patiently for the call that they had found Mia. Even the girls couldn't have fun, thinking she was gone. Her pillow lay cold at the side of the bed in the hope that it would be used again.

Mia hadn't thought of Nana or the sisters in hours. With all the distractions and threats from the kings' bodyguards and now possibly facing near death, how could she have? With a flick of her wrist her tiny claws shot out. And with a swing of her paw she cut through the bushes.

Suddenly the dark glow of the jungle turned to a blinding bright. Before her was the temple. The sun shone on it intensely. The temple itself was coated in gold and was magnificent to look at. She stood before the first section of a three-part staircase that led to the top. All over were statues of mankind with multiple arms holding many different coloured tools.

Some of them were fat men sitting with big smiles on their faces. Carvings on every wall showed the tiger hunting elephants and bears. Whoever had drawn them had respect for the tigers.

She proceeded up the tall staircase, getting closer and closer to the top. The excitement filled her heart as she was not sure what she was going to find. Finally she reached the top and slowly peered her head over the last step to avoid being spotted.

"Hummmmmm. Hummmmmm."

She heard a noise but wasn't sure what it was. Then there before her very eyes was a tiger. The more she looked the more of them she spotted. They were scattered all over the place. Sitting on their bottoms with their legs crossed like she had seen Nana sit. Some had their paws put together, others were pointing out. But they were all making the same hypnotic noise.

"Hummmmmm. Hummmmmm."

They appeared to be in some kind of trance. Unsure how to approach them, she thought asking for the leader would grab their attention. So she walked up to the closest tiger and tapped him softly with her paw.

"Um. Excuse me, could I speak with your king?"

"We are beings of light. We all follow the Buddha and, if she returns, the prophesized one," replied the tiger, who paid no attention to Mia.

"Well, is there anyone I could talk to? I've really travelled far just to ..." Abruptly she was interrupted.

"Alright, somebody get me some green tea, I've just lost all focus. Do you even know how deep I was?" He turned to Mia then paused for a brief second, "HAAAAAAAAAAAAAA! IT'S ... IT'S THE PROPHESIZED ONE!"

All attention turned to Mia. The tigers became frantic then ran to her and bowed down.

"The prophesized what?" she asked.

"We are not worthy, oh great one," said the tigers, who refused even to look Mia in the eye.

They remained at a bow. Every time she approached one to explain they moved back to keep their distance out of respect to her 'royal blood'.

"I just wanted to see the great tiger," Mia explained.

"Oh, but it is you that is great, oh wonderful Bastet, god of the cats and ruler of the temple."

"Oh no, I'm not," she replied.

"Oh, but you are," said one of the tigers, who stood up and pointed to a statue behind them.

There to the back, raised up high, was a statue of a small golden cat with a blue sapphire stone around its neck. It resembled a small village cat, as a matter of fact it looked very similar to Mia.

"You have returned as was prophesized, great one," he continued. "My servant name is Raphic. Would you like some green tea? Perhaps a pillow to rest on?"

"I'm not Bast …," she paused. "Well, actually I am rather hungry, some meat would go down great right now," she answered.

"Oh, but, your greatness, we only eat that which grows from the land," Raphic answered. "Roots, fruits, leaves, bark and berries."

Mia was shocked. These were not the tigers Bella had spoken of.

"I guess berries sounds good," she replied.

"Right away."

They surrounded her, picked her up and placed her on a pillow high up where she could see all.

"Tonight we celebrate your arrival," Raphic spoke excitedly. "For now you just sit back and relax."

To be honest, everything happened so fast Mia was speechless. She had turned vegetarian and become a god within a heartbeat. What was expected of her was uncertain. But the royal treatment was hard to push off. Suddenly she found herself playing the role.

"Excellent," she replied. Then placed her head on her new silk pillow that even had a picture of her on it. She watched over her new-found people as they prepared for the celebration.

The day started to fade into the night as Nana prepared to go to sleep. The girls were tucked in too, but all were going to sleep on an empty stomach. They couldn't eat if they thought Mia couldn't.

"Sleep well, Rose," said Edith. "Tomorrow I'm sure you'll find better news."

"Yes, you are probably right, I'm sure she's fine wherever she is. Goodnight," she replied.

Just below the temple lay Prince and Shootit, who were starting to get worried and impatient.

"I say, what if they've eaten her? Technically we wouldn't have to wait anymore," said Prince.

"Speaking of eating, I'm rather famished. We have to go and find something to eat before I go all pale and my coat goes dry," replied Shootit.

"But we said we would wait for her till morning. Wait a minute, do you hear that?"

"I say, I do. It sounds like drums. Do you think they're performing some kind of ritual before they eat her?"

"Well, the least we can do is watch. She will be missed though." The monkeys climbed through the bushes. Sneaked their way up the stairs and peered over.

"Wait, I can't look, that tiger carry-along accessory must be a limited edition collectors' item. Priceless. You look, Shootit. I just couldn't bear to watch!"

Shootit peered his head over but couldn't believe what he was seeing. "WHAT? No way!" he shouted.

"I knew it, it's worse than I thought." Prince continued to ramble on, not even realising that Shootit had got up and walked off. "What's happening, tell me more. Shootit, where are ..." Suddenly he became stunned with what his eyes were seeing. "WHAT? No way!"

Tigers were banging on drums, shaking shakers and dancing around a huge bonfire. With Mia as their guest of honour. Fresh fruit, berries and leaves were spread out everywhere. And obviously Shootit was heading towards it all.

"WAIT!" Prince shouted.

Suddenly the music stopped and everyone went quiet. All attention was on Prince. He looked around with a sad look on his face and then smiled with a tear in his eye.

"You all did this for me?" he said as he wiped his tear. The music started to play again and everyone turned back to what they were doing as if he wasn't even there.

"Prince," Mia shouted, "come here!"

"Oh hello, cat," Prince replied with a hint of bitterness.

"Hey, don't be such a downer, man. Tonight we celebrate the return of the great cat god Bastet," said two tigers as they picked Prince up and dragged him into the festivities.

"So cheer up and dance to the beat, little guy," said the other.

"Cat god?" he replied as he got pulled into the crowd. "That is a cat god?" he continued, looking at Mia.

Shootit and Prince gathered together near the fruits and berries and enjoyed the tigers' celebration. Mia, now starting to look the part, was surrounded by the female tigers, who covered her in jewellery and make-up they had made from the different berries they had picked.

As the moon moved overhead it had reached midnight. The music had stopped and the tigers had gathered around the mount Mia had been placed on. The oldest of the tigers, Kinshasa, approached the front. He had been around for many years and was one of the last of the tigers to know the real legend of Bastet. He began to tell the tale, all were silent in anticipation.

"Many, many centuries ago there lived a female of man who had been born from the God of the Sun. She was the goddess of the cat and protector of her people. Striking with the ferocity of the lion and the cunning of a tiger, she left fear in the hearts of all that opposed her. Regarded as a mother figure to all that worshipped her, Bastet ruled for many years. When she died they placed her in a tomb with 100,000 cats as guardian till the day she would return. Not as human but as cat and lead them as she once did the humans.

"And now finally she has returned," he concluded as he bowed before Mia.

Mia was in love with the story and believed it, so that she truly thought she could have been this great empress the tigers had been

41

waiting for. While they bowed and shouted out her name she began to lose the plot. Slowly her mind began to fade from its reality, not even thoughts of her dear old Nana or her sisters were able to get in. She had never felt so much appreciation from so many. Letting go of that was not on her mind.

When morning had arrived Prince and Shootit had returned from a little snooping they had done through the rest of the temple. Was it their curiosity about the tigers' strange behaviour or just hope that they would find something pretty to call their own? They tip-toed in-between the tigers, who were still fast asleep. They all lay around Mia, who was on her pillow. It looked like she was awake but not really there at all.

Prince looked in her eyes then in the direction she was looking. There was no response from her. "I say, Shootit, she appears to be zonked."

"You're the expert, Prince," replied Shootit.

Prince proceeded to snap his fingers in front of her but still no reply. Covered in all the make-up and jewellery, she almost looked like the statue of Bastet.

"I say, cat, are you there?" Shootit whispered in a concerned tone.

Suddenly she snapped out of it. "Prince, Shootit, what can I do for you today?" she answered with a rather high grace about herself.

"Mia, we've been scratching around, well, more like searching for …," Shootit was interrupted by Prince.

"No, we've noticed some of the drawings on the temple walls lower down. These tigers aren't meant to be here in this temple."

"How dare you," she replied. "This is the temple of Bastet, the cat god, which happens to be me. And I say they are."

"Just come and look," replied Prince.

Down the long stairs they went, to the inner parts of the temple where the tigers never seemed to venture. There the walls were covered in hundreds of paintings that appeared to tell a story.

42

"Look, these paintings were drawn by men. It shows that they once lived here until one day the tigers ventured up into the temple and chased man away," explained Prince.

"And over here, drawings of the tiger in the jungle with the elephants and bears bowing to them," continued Shootit.

"That's why there are so many gangs in the jungle. The tigers used to be the kings but since they've been up in this temple they've forgotten their old ways," said Prince.

"But what about Bastet and the legend of her returning to lead them?" she asked.

"Well, if you truly are then it's up to you to lead them back into the jungle where they belong, so the gang wars can end and peace be restored," Prince explained. "It's been ages since we could travel where we pleased in the jungle without fearing for our lives. You have to try at least."

"You're right, I don't know what I was thinking. I believed we would stay up here happily ever after with me as their god. I'd forgotten I even had a family to get back to. It's time to fix this." They raced up to the top where the tigers had gathered together.

"Ah, Bastet, where did you go? We thought something had happened to you," shouted Raphic.

"I'm quite fine. But I have something to say to you all. You must all move back into the jungle and stop the gangs."

"Ha, ha, ha," they laughed. "Mia, we are beings of peace. We do not involve ourselves with gangs, and it is forbidden that we leave your temple," they replied.

"This isn't my temple or Bastet's temple. And if we don't leave and sort out the jungle the smaller animals will never have a chance to live there again."

"Enough, we must all return to meditation and forget this conversation ever took place," Kinshasa demanded. Although Mia was considered to be a god he still had authority over the tigers. "I do not wish to challenge you but we will never be led into war against the other animals even if it is you that requests it," he continued.

"If you don't have the courage to take your rightful place in the jungle then that's fine, but don't hide behind gods and excuses so you can feel better about your decisions," Mia shouted.

Kinshasa stopped with his back turned to her but seemed to take offence to what she had said.

"I thought the tigers were fierce creatures that were respected by the animals. I won't be a god to cowards," she said, "I guess we'll find another way to help."

Mia, Prince and Shootit headed out of the temple and back into the thick bush of the dense jungle. Not sure what she would do next was becoming a regular thought for Mia. But if anything she knew from the past, it was that something would come along to show the way. Halfway back into the jungle Prince decided it was time to share his thoughts. With another tear dripping from his eye he spoke.

"Well, I'm just so proud of you standing up to those tigers the way you did. Now that that's out of the way you must be mad in the head if you think we're stepping into that jungle after what happened last time! And worse, now we don't even have backup! What were you thinking? I think I'm going to have a heart attack." Shootit ran over to Prince as he faked a faint.

"Keep it together, man, or, or I might just faint as well … Oh!" Shootit replied.

"*Shootit*, come back to me, it'll be alright, I'll let the bears eat me first," pleaded Prince who had snapped out of his panic attack.

"You will?" replied Shootit. "Well then, no use lying on the floor."

"Oh, would you both be quiet! I need to think," Mia demanded.

"Well, look who it is. My little friends have returned to the jungle. I hope you haven't forgotten our little deal?"

A pale pair of monkeys suddenly lost the ability to speak. The grizzly bear had returned.

"We have no gift for you, bear, not for you and not for your king," Mia replied.

"Well, that's interesting because I was hoping you didn't." He moved in on the three of them and cornered them by a tree.

"Now, I don't like to mix meat when I eat, but today I'm going to make an exception. Ha, ha, ha, ha."

Mia and the monkeys were frightened beyond horror, as they quivered in their fur. Somehow Shootit grew a pair of legs. He shot off in the direction of the temple, leaving the other two behind.

"No matter, two will still be enough until I find you, coward," shouted the bear. "No more games."

Suddenly a violent roar came from another bear in the distance. "The elephants are attacking Amul. Let's teach them a lesson they'll never forget!" the bear growled and then ran off. "You two are lucky this time, but I'll be back for you." Off he went to join the rest of the army.

"Let's get out of here now!" screamed Prince.

"No, we have to try and stop them from destroying the forest, Prince," she replied and then ran off.

"You can't be serious. Are you insane?" he asked, with no effort to follow. Watching as she disappeared into the distance. Following the noise of the ground shaking, Mia found herself near the edge of a hill overlooking the bears and the elephants.

"This is our jungle and we'll have no bears roaming around it without our permission," shouted the elephants.

"This jungle belongs to Amul, king of the jungle!" shouted the bears.

"Wait!" Mia shouted. "Why can't the jungle belong to everyone?"

"It's you!" shouted the elephant that had let them pass. "We'll deal with you when we're finished with these bears. ELEPHANTS, ATTACK!"

The bears and the elephants engaged in war, shaking the ground so that it had brought Mia off the edge of the hill and right in between it all. And if that wasn't enough, from high above in the trees came tumbling down a troop of monkeys that had decided they too had a right to ownership. Chaos broke loose as trees were bashed down and sand was blown everywhere. Mia was certain she was going to be stomped on, trying to miss all the animals as they attacked one another.

A large elephant was raised onto its hind legs to push a bear over but looked as if it was going to crush Mia. Everything slowed down as her life started to flash before her very eyes. Again thoughts of her old Nana and her sisters were on her mind.

Why had she gone to look for those tigers instead of finding her way home to them? Down came the mighty leg of the elephant right over her head. Paralyzed from fear, she could only watch …

More dust flew into her eyes and now she could not see the elephant, but expected to feel the stomp on her. Nothing, but a shake of the ground and a roar so loud she lost all hearing for a brief moment. The dust began to fade and there before her were the tigers. To the side of her was the elephant lying on his side. Shootit and Prince came riding in on the back of Raphic, screaming at the top of their voices, they raced into the battlefield.

Kinshasa stepped in front as the tigers surrounded the jungle animals, who had now realised they were in a bit of trouble. Then he spoke.

"The King of the Jungle has returned, and if you have a problem with that you are going to have to take it up with my army," he shouted. "Anyone interested?"

The animals were quiet and afraid. They moved back from the tigers, bowed once then turned back into the depths of the jungle.

The tigers then turned to Mia to take their bow.

"Wait!" she yelled. "I'm not Bastet, you don't need to bow to me," she explained.

"Oh, but you are," replied Kinshasa. "We had been in that temple for so long we had forgotten what it really meant to be a tiger. You came and led us back to who we were, as prophesized. You are our protector, Bastet."

Finding it hard not to be seduced by the idea of being a god, Mia knew it was time for the fantasy to end. She had journeyed enough for one little cat and started to feel her heart calling her to a place she had neglected while in the jungle. It was time to go back to her Nana and three sisters.

But how? She had no idea how she had even arrived in the jungle and where she would find her family.

"Kinshasa, all of you are welcome in my heart but this is not where my journey ends," she said.

"What do you mean? Where does it end?" he replied.

The tigers looked up with a touch of sadness, they had waited so long to find Bastet they weren't ready to let go. Even if she wasn't they had found something that gave their beliefs substance.

"I must find my protector, I suppose," she tried to explain. "But I'm not sure how."

"Hold it! Prince," He then pushed through the tigers to the front with Shootit following. Once again he had all attention on him. He paused for a moment as he looked around and then he spoke.

"I am the protector," he proclaimed. The excitement on Mia's faced dropped to a dull disappointment, along with everyone else who knew from experience that Prince's words had very little truth behind them. "What?" he asked, trying to look hurt. "Really I am. Mia, come to me. I am your protector."

"We don't know where you came from but we know a human that might able to help," said Shootit as he interrupted Prince's babble. "She helped us during the turf wars. Maybe she can help you. She lives on a small farm not too far from here," he continued.

"Sure, if you're a *tiger* maybe," argued Prince.

"Well then, you've got plenty of those," said Kinshasa. "We'll take you there with no bears or elephants getting in your way."

"Oh please. That would be much appreciated," Mia replied with a touch of desperation in her voice.

"Tigers, you heard Bastet. Let's move!" Kinshasa ordered.

And so off they went, racing through the jungle. The tigers ran with all their might while Mia and the monkeys held onto their backs. They were going so fast they even caught up with the elephants that

47

they had just fought with. Thinking the tigers had come back to punish them, they started to climb the trees to get away.

Woooosh!

A sound that brought a sigh of relief as they watched the tigers pass them by. Mia had never had so much fun in her entire life. She began to smile as she realised no village cat had ever seen or done as much as she had. She felt privileged.

Not far away on a little farm, Nana lay asleep out at the back. She had tried to knit to take her mind off Mia but didn't get too far. Bella, Linky and Coco sat around her chair, trying to pull the wool off Nana's lap. Her mind was filled with guilt so that even her dreams were of Mia. She blamed herself for taking them along and wished she'd never even come.

Suddenly a weight came onto her lap that shocked her into waking up. There, sitting on her lap, was Mia.

"Meow," said Mia.

"Mia? Mia, how did you get back here? Where have you been, my little angel?"

It had turned out the human that helped them was Edith, Nana's friend.

Nana was so shocked that she was calm and didn't even jump up. The empty feeling was full again and she was more than happy just to rub Mia the way she used to. All the sisters gathered around asking millions of questions when a loud roar came from far away.

The tigers and Mia's monkey protectors stood on a hill in the distance. Nana and the sisters were frightened. But there was no need. They were just saying goodbye to their friend.

Mia screeched her loudest 'meow' then rolled into a ball in Nana's lap and fell to sleep. Nana and the girls were so shocked and confused but felt she had earned a good sleep before they bothered her with that one.

How they got home in the end? Well, that's another story.

RACE FOR
THE NILE

TWO YEARS AND SEVENTEEN DAYS had passed since Mia had ventured through to India. She had grown considerably and was becoming an adult. Not much else had changed in the small village she lived in. Nana still enjoyed sitting on her rocking chair, knitting away as she matured into her old age. The three sisters, Bella, Linky and Coco, had grown close to Mia and spent much of their time sitting around, enjoying the sun rise and set. Sleeping most of the days away, only getting up for a nibble of tuna.

Mia had grown into the same lazy habits that all village cats have when becoming an adult. There wasn't really much else to do in their village. There was no competing with each other, no turf wars and no thick jungles to claw their way through. They truly lived the good life with very little to worry about.

Despite that Mia was quite the adventurer in her teenage days; it seemed that she too had lost interest in venturing beyond her own front gate. Had the jungles of Africa and India worn her out? One could only guess. She might have given up on the jungle but it seemed the jungle was certainly not ready to let her go …

It was a dark night in the village, so dark the moon itself struggled to give light. Clouds gathered around to block its glow, giving shade to all below. It looked as if something was controlling them to hide its presence. It was a warm night, the air moist but there was a breeze that brought a chill to the town's spine. All was quiet. It appeared that all was fast asleep or hiding and did not want to be heard. Something was different, something only the animals would have noticed. A scent of some sort that was so faint man himself would not be able to smell it.

It reeked of an animal that had just been in a kill. Drenched in the blood of its prey, it raced in-between the shadows of the village searching, looking, sniffing. A glimpse of two eyes glowed red and was then gone. It was trying to move as quietly as possible, not to be heard by anyone, and yet its claws scraped against the tar roads so loudly they struck fear into any animal that heard them.

What was this strange presence and what was its purpose in the village? Time would only tell.

Not far away, lay Mia and her sisters all snuggled up together deep in slumber. They were not aware of the intruder that had sneaked into their little town. Free of fear and free of nightmares they snored away, dreaming of butterflies and rainbows. Mia was dreaming of herself as the cat god of the tigers, hoping it would one day be a reality again.

SCRATCH … TAP … TAP …

These noises made no sense in her dream, why were they here? Suddenly she jumped up, realising she was really hearing it. What was it and why was it interrupting her well-earned sleep? She proceeded to the window but could see nothing. So she flipped the handle and leaped outside to investigate.

She approached the tree that she had used to escape from the garden, when suddenly she was startled. Something very large was sitting on the other side with its back to her. Uncertain of what to do next she decided to move closer to work out what it was she was looking at. Her heart began to beat harder with every step she took.

"Hello, Mia," said a deep voice. One she was certain she had never heard before and yet it seemed to know who she was.

"Who is that? I mean, hello," she replied, trying not to be rude. "Do I know you?"

The voice turned its face to look at her. Its red eyes shone brightly but its face seemed troubled. It spoke again while walking to a different place in the garden where the moon shed more light.

"Has it been that long, old friend? I suppose I have changed a lot over the years although you still look the same. I guess he was right about that." With very little eye contact he continued to stare up at the moon, appearing very troubled and down.

"Lusark? Is that … you?" she said.

"The one and only," he replied, still looking disturbed.

Mia proceeded to move towards him to get a better look at him. She was almost frightened by his appearance. He had grown a lot since she had last seen him. He had even grown a mane although not as big as his father's. What scared her most were the scars that had accumulated on his body and face.

It was all fun and games for them and life was a lot simpler when they were young. It seemed the jungle had a way of taking that away and forcing one to grow up rather fast. The only scar Mia had was from slipping and falling out of a tree one day. She didn't want to be the last one to get to dinner and had lost control. To be honest, it wasn't even one worth mentioning. A lifetime of things had happened between them and she was seconds away from hearing just how much.

Still speechless, she tried to break the ice. "What's wrong? You don't seem yourself." Mia had a way with spotting when something was wrong, or perhaps it was because lions never leave the jungle, that she was concerned.

There was still no life in his face but one tear escaped from his eyelid. He spoke. "It's all too much to even try and explain, but I'll do my best." He took her back into the past as he explained how he had arrived at that very spot. All the lions were gathered around the King at the top of the valley. He was preparing for a challenge that would give him the right to be king of the African jungle. It was very secretive and was only known amongst the toughest and strongest of predators in the jungle.

Every decade the African predators would compete on an endurance course from the Kalahari Desert all the way to the top of Africa along the Nile and into Egypt. The winner was deemed king of the African jungle amongst all that roamed it.

The lions were the reigning champions and had never been defeated. Despite this, the other predators never gave up. In fact, it made them so bitter that they had reached a point where they would have done anything to take the throne away. Even cheat. The rules were that only the leader of each group could compete and he could choose one partner to accompany him.

If the groups crossed each others' paths while on the race they would fight one another. Obviously the winner would continue forward. The aim was to avoid being spotted by the other groups and to choose the simplest and fastest of routes. From there the jungle itself left many challenges never seen before that they would have to conquer. In the end they would need to be the first to find the Egyptian Siamese cats, who were the judges and were considered to be the illuminati of the animal underworld.

This time around it was Lusark's father and one of his brave bodyguards who would do the course. He spoke his last words before starting the race.

"My people, it is an honour to defend the lions' title to the throne. I will make you all proud, and when I return we shall all eat as kings."

That was the last the pride had ever seen of their king. He was ambushed by all the other predators in the race and was put to rest on the very day he left.

Lusark continued to explain. "As heir to the throne I was the new king, but the pride was not sure I was mature enough to take on the responsibility. I struggled to deal with losing my father and with all the pressure from the pride to continue the challenge I took off. You were the only one I knew I could count on. After what I have done I don't think they'll ever accept me back again."

Mia placed her paw on his shoulder for comfort, but could not hold back a tear or two from her own eyes. She wasn't sure what to say to make him feel better. If truth be told, there were no words that could have brought peace to his thoughts. They stared up at the sky together and enjoyed the peace of the early morning. The sun was beginning to rise over the village, which wasn't a good thing for anyone who saw a lion sitting in Nana's backyard. Mia had to help Lusark. That was certain, but how? Then it all came together in a blink of an eye.

"I know!" she exclaimed. Lusark turned to her in disbelief. "We have to finish the race," she continued.

"Mia, it's impossible, do you have any idea how to get to Egypt? And with all the other predators looking out for any lions that crossed their path, we would never be able to get through," Lusark replied.

"Think of it. The other lions will take you back if you win the challenge. And what better way to honour your father than completing what he started? Finding how to get there, I've learnt, is an answer you'll only receive when you're lost," she answered.

"Mia, you truly are a brave cat," replied Lusark. He started to smile as he realised a way out of his problems. Maybe one he always knew, but under no pressure from the tribe he could see it for the first time. "Well, considering they've got two days' head start we had better get going." Lusark jumped up the tree and over the wall.

SMASH!

Nana was an early riser and made a cup of tea before coming outside to watch the sun rise. Obviously she wasn't prepared to see a lion jumping over the wall. But she had started to work out that Mia was a more than average cat with more than average friends. Mia looked back and meowed.

"Go, little one, you know where to find me," she said. Mia purred to Nana then proceeded after Lusark over the wall. Nana began to laugh as her heart started to slow down to normal. "I tell you, that cat is going to be the end of me," she laughed to herself as she walked back inside.

Lusark raced through the village streets as fast as he could while the sun chased from behind. Mia had taken her place on his back, holding on tight to his mane. The now waking dogs in the village howled violently as if to say they were not scared. But they were ...

Mia hadn't had such a rush of excitement for two years. It was good to be back, she thought to herself. They raced at top speeds but to where was uncertain. Lusark had decided Mia was right. They would deal with it when they got there.

The journey had just begun for Mia and Lusark, who were already two days behind the other predators. The predators, with the cheetahs leading the way, had just passed the rocky pathway and were over the border of South Africa. The cheetahs' advantage was their ability to run faster than any other animal in the desert. They were light and very stealthy – picking up speeds of 120 kilometres per hour, where all that could be seen of them was the dust they left behind.

Not far behind though were the leopards, who weren't as fast but made up for it in strength. Followed by the hyenas, who lacked both strength and speed but more than made up for it in their determination to win at any cost. Their focus was to eliminate the competition and walk to victory.

"Hurry up," groaned Sirus, the leader of the hyenas. "The kingdom is mine for the taking."

"Yes, master," replied his loyal servant, if ever you could find a loyal one amongst hyenas.

"We'll catch them at the pass and wipe those cats out once and for all," Sirus stated as his huge paws dug into the ground, pulling his large misshapen body along.

Racing far behind were Mia and Lusark. Still, in the Kalahari Desert Lusark found comfort. It was his own turf and he had no problem catching up, using the short cuts his father had taught him.

The afternoon sun beat hard over the desert, finally slowing the race down to a moderate pace. This was the time the leopards' strength would prevail over the cheetahs, who did not have the natural stamina to maintain their high speeds. Always dragging behind though were the hyenas hungry for victory. The sun was not hot enough to discourage them because they were tough creatures of the desert.

Water would soon be a very important possession for anyone who wanted to keep the lead. And of course the hunger of a predator would soon slow them down when having to hunt their prey. Many of the challengers from before had even been injured during the hunt and found themselves having to forfeit. Somehow the lions had found a method of surviving and had excelled at it.

Unfortunately Lusark had never been given a chance to learn it from his own father. Every step he took out of the Kalahari Desert was new territory for him. Uncertain of what was to come next, they enjoyed their last glimpse of the sun as it waved its goodbyes for the night.

"I think we need to rest for the night so we can get an early start to the morning," suggested Mia as she found comfort on a nearby rock.

"You're right," Lusark replied. "We have no water, nor food. Tomorrow will be a tough day for us. Let's just get some sleep …," but before he could finish his sentence they had both passed out.

The race had just started and already things weren't looking too good for the duo. What would happen if they crossed one of the other packs? With Mia's small size she would never be able to help Lusark in a fight.

And when Lusark's animal hunger kicked in, how would it affect their relationship? Mia was clearly uncomfortable with hunting other animals. In India she had even eaten berries for a short time. Despite that she had never had to fend for her own food. Would her own hunger eventually take over her beliefs? For the African jungle had very little fruit and berries …

The leopards and cheetahs had also turned in for the night, but the race was still on for the hyenas. Whether it was raw determination or pure stupidity for not getting their rest they carried on through the night. They needed a decent lead if their plan to take out the competition was to work.

"Hawwooooooooooo," howled Sirus's loyal servant as he stared up at the moon.

"You idiot! What are you doing? If the others hear us they'll know we're ahead and will be expecting us," shouted Sirus.

"I'm sorry, I can't help it. Every time it's full moon something just comes over me and I have to howl," the servant replied.

"Did I mention what an idiot you are?" Sirus replied. "I swear if you mess this up for me I will take you over to the gorge of crocodile pit and throw you right into it. Now mush."

Close into the early morning, after having reached a considerable distance, the hyenas came to rest at the top of Dead Man's Peak. It was a short cliff overlooking the northern pathway. It was called Dead Man's Peak because, if you stood on the top of it, in the distance you could see Crocodile Gorge. If you squinted your eyes it almost looked as if they could walk right into it.

Sirus had a different plan for it though. One that involved pushing a large rock over it as the other predators passed under it, blocking the pathway and possibly even hurting the others. To him he had already won, all he needed to do was get rid of some flies on the way. Old Sirus was truly the most ruthless leader the jungle had ever seen.

The race was on again for the other predators, who had woken up at the crack of dawn. The leopards were catching up with the cheetahs at top speed and were on the verge of passing them. To avoid having to fight them they took a higher route that gave them a better overview of what was to come. Mia and Lusark had an hour's head start but were still far behind. Tracing paw prints and leftover kill they found on their way. With little hope in their hearts and the dying need to make it up to his father they pushed on through high grounds and low, finding themselves surrounded by a vast piece of Africa they had never seen before.

"Lusark, are you alright? You haven't said much in a while."

Lusark's hunger had started to eat at him for the first time on their journey. The true beast of the lion was coming out of him. His face was still – focused on what was for lunch.

"I'm fine, just a little tired, I guess," he replied. He was well aware of Mia's feelings on hunting other animals and did not want to upset her. He decided he would wait until dark if possible.

The high speeds of the cheetahs had them smiling at one another as they watched their competition stray behind.

"This is too easy," laughed Shesha, the leader of the cheetahs. His name was a Zulu phrase that meant 'fast one'. It was for one simple reason, he was really fast. "With the lions out of the way the throne is ours."

"If we can keep this pace we'll be in Egypt in no time," replied his younger brother Uthuli, whose Zulu name meant 'dust', for the simple reason that if you raced with him that's all you would see. He was not as fast as his older brother but they never competed with one another to know.

Unfortunately for the two their arrogance was going to be their downfall, as they were not aware of the hyenas waiting for them ahead. And with the cloud of dust that was dragging up behind them they were quite easy to spot from Dead Man's Peak.

"Your Royal Highness, awake! I see dust clouds in the distance."

Sirus was not one to be around when he woke, but good news always put him in a brightened mood.

"EXCELLENT! If I'm not mistaken it must be those pesky cheetahs. Think they've taken the lead, do they? Ha, ha, ha, ha, ha. It's like I always say, he who sleeps last laughs longest. Now let's get this rock ready for its opening show."

As the cheetahs moved along the narrow pathway that led under Dead Man's Peak, Uthuli started to slow down. Something didn't seem right but he wasn't sure what it was.

"Come on, bro, we need this lead if we want to sleep in peace tonight," shouted Shesha. "Keep up with me."

Uthuli came to a complete stop as he watched his brother move into the distance. The narrow passage had a dark, cold feel to it the further it led in. But there was a smell that he couldn't avoid. It was the scent of another animal that had marked its territory.

"But it's not possible," he said to himself, trying to deny his instincts. "None of the other predators could have overtaken us, could they?"

After almost convincing himself that everything was fine, he noticed something on the very edge of the path leading up the side of it. His face dropped and his heart stopped a beat. It was the print of a hyena's paw and that meant only one thing. Suddenly he broke out into a sprint after Shesha, who had disappeared from sight.

"Shesha, wait, it's a trap!" he screamed.

The ground started to shake with a large crashing sound ahead. He couldn't see what it was but it didn't sound good. Then as he came around the bend, the sight was one that stopped him in his tracks.

A boulder so big he couldn't even see his brother under it, but he knew. Time seemed to stop, all he could hear was his heart pounding in his chest and the tears as they dropped to the floor.

"No," he squeaked. "Not now and not like this, brother."

Uthuli broke out into a roar of anger that echoed all the way back to Mia and Lusark. He looked up to the top of the creek and couldn't believe what he saw. The same two hyenas he had teamed with to ambush the lion king were the same two that had ambushed his brother. Karma had come back to bite them when they had least expected.

"I'll get you, hyenas," he shouted.

"Just let that be a lesson to you," Sirus replied. "The kingdom is mine. Best you pass that on to those leopards if you don't want the same fate for them."

The hyenas ran off to complete the race, while Uthuli sat back in shock. He couldn't believe how his own selfish actions had brought him so much pain. Unsure of what to do next, he turned away from the race and drifted into the jungle.

These were the consequences of the challenge and the raw truth of the African jungle. There were no certainties and no second chances. Unlike the first time Mia had stepped foot into the jungle, when she was lucky to have stepped out alive. This was a whole new version of its wrath.

Were these two young and naïve creatures ready for the challenge? Earning the right to rulership over the jungle was no game.

"Did you hear that, Lusark?" asked a very frightened Mia.

"It sounded like a cheetah. But that wasn't a normal roar, Mia, I think something has happened. Best we keep a lookout," he replied.

"Well, at least we know we're close to the competition," she said. "Whether that's a good thing or not we will never know."

"Right, well, we had best get a move on before nightfall and find some shelter," Lusark replied.

Mia climbed on Lusark's back so they could speed things up as they raced through the long grass towards the valley that led beneath Dead Man's Creek. Despite that the hyenas had already left there was still reason for concern. Crocodile Gorge was just beyond that point and was certainly going to be a challenge to get around.

Another night had come to pass over the race and already so much had been lost. Fathers and brothers had been laid to rest and many had been deceived by ones they believed they could trust.

The leopards had gained some ground but were unaware of the hyenas' lead. They still believed the cheetahs were in the race. Uthuli had found a place to rest in a nearby cave, hoping sleep would come along swiftly so he could stop feeling the hurt for his brother, even just for a moment. He wasn't sure what he was to do next and really didn't seem to care.

Mia and Lusark found comfort under a nearby Baobab tree that resembled the one the pride used to lie under when they had first met. It wasn't hard to get to sleep from there for poor old Mia, who had never done so much travelling in such a short time.

This was an opportunity for Lusark to get away and find some prey to feed his hunger. He got up quietly and sneaked away into the dark, using his nose as a tracking tool for any nearby kudu.

As per usual, still awake and still moving further ahead were the ever determined hyenas.

"We've finally reached Crocodile Gorge," yelled Sirus. "We can rest here, my pet, while I plan the next sabotage for any of those who still think they have a right to my throne. Crocodile Gorge is an inspiration for all that is devious," he boasted.

"Is that you, oh wise and evil one?" shouted a sinister voice from the trees above.

"What? Who's there? Show yourself before I show you how evil I can be," replied Sirus, who to be honest was more afraid of the voice than anything else. Sirus was afraid of most things, including his own shadow, and so had to compete with everything in order to hide his own true fears.

"We have heard much of you and would like to make an alliance of some sort," continued the voice.

"Yes … I'm listening," he replied.

"We hear you are set to take the throne and we only wish to help in return for a small compensation."

"Why don't you show yourself before I listen any further?" Sirus became impatient, as did all hyenas when they had to pay attention for anything longer than a moment.

"As you wish."

Suddenly the trees began to shake at their branches until a strange-looking creature appeared, hanging upside down.

"A bat. Ha. Why should I have any use for a furry little bat?"

"Do not mock me, for I can be your best friend and your worst enemy," it replied. "We can track down your competition and lead them in the wrong direction."

"And what do I give you in return for this 'favour'?" he asked.

"Just what is ours, in livestock and land. A very noble request if I do say so myself."

"Fine, fine, find them and misguide them. Even though I don't really need your help. I've got rid of the lions," he answered in an arrogant tone.

"Oh you have, but a lion still follows your tracks," the bat replied.

"WHAT! Impossible. I got rid of their king. They have no leader and so they cannot compete."

"It's not the King that chases you, but his son Lusark who has taken the leadership and wishes to gain the throne for the lions."

"Lusark. Ha, ha, ha, ha. I have no reason to fear that kitten," Sirus answered with a laugh. But remembering that he quietly even feared his own shadow, he adjusted his attitude. "Yes, yes, if you must then lead him away and I will grant you what you wish, but know this, bat, mess me around and it will be you who will need to get lost."

The one thing Mia had always to look forward to was the fact that every time she went to sleep she would fall into a beautiful dream. However, since Lusark had come back into her life this was fast becoming a passing phase. She was again dreaming of butterflies and yet the noises they were making were not making any sense. Suddenly she jumped up.

"Not again," she said. This time there was no Lusark around her, just the cold hum of the jungle breeze and the creeps and squeaks of the insects that lived in it.

"Lusark?" she shouted, but there was no response. Concerned, she got up and moved on to look for him. Following the faint noises she heard in her sleep.

"There you are," she said quietly as she moved up from behind him. No response from Lusark, it almost seemed like déjà vu all over again.

"Lusark," she said. Her heart beating fast like before. Was it him or some other lion she had inconveniently sneaked up on in her half-awake, half-asleep stroll? As she came around the front she noticed that it was him, only he was quiet because he was eating some prey he had just caught. Ashamed of what she would think, he looked down.

"Mia, this may not be normal for you but it is how I live in the jungle. How all predators have to live. I tried to hide it from you but I have to eat," he said. "We need our strength out here or we'll never survive, Mia, you need to realise that," he continued.

"I don't know what to say right now, I'm going back to sleep," she answered. As she turned away she spoke again. "I'm not disappointed in you. I'm just confused as to how I feel about that. Goodnight, Lusark."

Unsure as to how she felt about hunting other animals, Mia climbed up next to the tree and tried to go back to sleep. Her hunger was starting to get to her too, and she wasn't sure what she would find to make a meal. Tuna was so conveniently served from a can back home. Maybe she was going to have to let go of certain opinions when morning came.

Unfortunately for them a weakness was spotted by an ever watchful eye. For the bat had seen their dispute and was very much planning to exploit it.

"Ahum," said the bat, who was hanging upside down from a branch. "Ahum!" it continued, trying to get Mia's attention. "You there," it whispered, trying not to be heard by Lusark.

"Who said that?" she asked.

"Up here, silly girl. I see your selfish friend wishes to force you to eat meat or starve to death," it replied.

"No, he doesn't, there's not much else to eat out here so I guess eventually I too will have to eat the meat of a buck," she answered.

"Nonsense!" the bat screeched. "There is plenty of fruit to eat from the land just down that way. Why has he not told you, when all the jungle animals know this?"

"Lusark wouldn't lie to me, I'm almost sure of it," she answered, seeming very unsure.

"Well, if you follow me I'll show you how selfish he really is. Forcing you to eat another poor animal. It's barbaric, but I expect no less from a lion. He thinks only with his stomach. Come along, follow me, I'll show you."

The bat led the way as Mia followed him into the dark. She had forgotten that she could not trust anyone in the jungle. Let alone a bat, which was the most devious of all the creatures there.

"Come see," it said. "Plenty of fruit for you to eat." He had led her to the edge of a short cliff.

"Where? I see nothing," she replied.

"Oh, poor child, I forget us bats see rather well in the dark. Step a little closer and then maybe you shall see," he continued to persuade her closer to the edge. She moved a little closer and started to squint her eyes in the hope that she would see better.

"I still see no fruit," she replied.

"WELL THEN, LOOK A LITTLE CLOSER!" the bat screamed as he pushed Mia over the cliff. "HA, HA, HA, HA, HA. YOU SILLY FOOL!"

Mia rolled down, further and further over rocks and tree roots, until finally she reached the bottom. There she lay unconscious.

What was to become of her was very uncertain, and how would Lusark react when he found out she was no longer there? He had finished eating as morning began to spread through the dark. Lusark made his way back up to the Baobab tree where Mia had gone to sleep. But she was not there. He wasn't sure what to think but started to get worried. Help, however, was there to guide him.

"Are you looking for that little village cat?" said the bat, who had taken his place back on the tree branch.

"Yes, have you seen her?" he asked.

"Sure, sure, she was very upset with you for eating that buck. Her last words, I believe, were, I'm heading home."

"What? I can't believe she would … Fine, if she can't understand then she was never meant to be here in the first place," Lusark answered.

"I couldn't agree more. Things are truly different in the jungle, maybe too much for a village cat to understand," the bat replied, trying to agree with Lusark's irrational thoughts.

"Thank you for your help," he said to the bat and then turned away to continue the race on his own. Disappointed and rather sad, things looked worse with every step he took. However, he was not going to give up. "I'm going to win for my father!" he shouted.

While Lusark bolted off to the horizon poor Mia had just started to wake up from her violent fall. Her vision was not right and, even worse; she did not know where she was.

"Lusark," she cried out.

With no sign of him she staggered on, praying she had not lost her friend.

"Lusark," she shouted again. "Where are you? Can you hear me?"

A voice replied but it was not Lusark. Still, it was something to her in her moment of desperation.

"Lusark the lion?" the voice asked. "Lusark's in the race?"

Still unable to see where the voice was coming from she replied, "Yes, Lusark the lion. Yes, he's in the race, if it's the same race we're talking about. But I've lost him."

Suddenly Uthuli stepped out from a dark and hollow cave.

"If Lusark is in the race then there is still a chance for me to make it up to his family," he said. "We have to find him before the hyenas do."

"Wait a minute," Mia replied. "You're one of the predators that ambushed Lusark's father. Why should I trust you? If anything you'll probably try to take Lusark out too."

"That is true. It's not something I'm proud of. I have already paid the price of my actions. And now all I want is to make things right. Just give me a chance to prove it."

"Well I don't have much of a choice. I have no idea where I am. So I guess 'Where do we start?' would be the next question," she replied with a certain cheeky tone to her voice.

"We'll have to head for Crocodile Gorge and pray we get to him before anyone else does."

Mia followed the cheetah in the hope that his word was true and that she could find her friend once again. At this point it seemed the cheetah's intentions were good but she was no longer in the game for trusting strangers.

Forgetting that she had an empty stomach, her body was running weak and would eventually slow the cheetah down. She knew she had to eat. But what?

Further up the leopards had just reached Crocodile Gorge but were rather surprised to see the hyenas waiting at the riverbed and not the cheetahs. They too were aware of the hyenas' devious nature but weren't sure whether an instinct was enough to act on.

They decided that to avoid conflict they would swim across the gorge further down from them. Remember, it wasn't the ones who could fight the best but the ones who could get through fastest without being noticed that stood the best chance to win.

The hyenas hadn't noticed the leopards as they began their long swim across Crocodile Gorge. The leopards climbed in too and began their journey through. But one thing didn't make sense. Why were there no crocodiles to try and stop them in Crocodile Gorge? And why did they seem so confident as they swam across?

It certainly wasn't because they were stronger, for the crocodile was the most ferocious and most powerful creature in all the jungles in the world. Its mighty jaws were strong enough to crush even an elephant and its skin was so tough not even a lion's bite could penetrate it. Surely they would have had some concern. Or perhaps they knew something not many did. Finally they reached the other side, unharmed and eager to continue the race.

Feeling rather proud of himself, Lusark's instinct guided him with ease. He thought to himself, I'm pretty good at this. This isn't such a tough race. Or so he thought ... For arrogance in the jungle never goes down well. "Crocodile Gorge," he shouted. He had heard of it in stories passed around in his youth but wasn't sure what all the hype was about. From a quick glance it was really quite plain. He had seen many waterholes before, perhaps this one was bigger but there was no real cause for concern in his eyes.

Little did he know it was moments like these that turned lion cubs into lion kings. Any experienced predator had a heightened sense for noticing what was and what wasn't around him. And the fact that there were no other animals around to be seen would have been a dead giveaway.

Not listening to the advice from the elders given to him when he was a cub. "Never cross Crocodile Gorge unless you are with one who knows it. Rather walk around it." This was now going to be his second mistake.

But time was short and he had no real reason not to just swim across it. Perhaps his luck would be the same as the others. He took his first step and dipped his paw in the water but then immediately withdrew it. He started to laugh at himself and then boldly plunged into the depths of the brown, slimy water.

Unfortunately for Lusark luck would not be on his side through this journey. For all experienced predators knew that crocodiles leave the water at midday to warm themselves up. That was the time the hyenas and leopards crossed. But midday had passed and the crocodiles had returned to their slumps.

"Ha, ha," he laughed. "This isn't so bad at all," he said to himself, before noticing that he was being followed. Not by one or two or three but by four crocodiles. This was the first time Lusark had experienced true fear. His heart started to beat faster as he broke out into a panic. Pawing his way as hard as he could to reach the other side. Suddenly his arrogance had turned into deep respect. This was no longer his turf.

Faster and faster he swam away, but the crocodiles were excellent swimmers and were not ready to give up such a large dinner. Closer and closer came the sounds of the crocodiles' chomping jaws.

Lusark swam for his life but finally one got hold of his leg. Sharp edges grazed into him as the jaw closed down. He hadn't given up yet for he had almost reached the other side. He kept pawing and pulling but the crocodile's weight had slowed him down and the others were beginning to catch up. If they got to him he would certainly be doomed. Luckily for him, his little friend was near and as always she had other friends.

Uthuli roared his heart out to catch the attention of the crocodiles. But that wasn't enough to turn them away. Lusark was a sure thing and the crocodiles hated to gamble. After one last desperate attempt at a roar he decided there was no other choice but to give them what they wanted.

Uthuli plunged into the water and then gave off another roar. Luckily for Lusark, crocodiles also despised sharing and thought Uthuli was a fair trade. While Lusark broke his way free on the other side Uthuli swiftly jumped back out of the water. Crocodiles were a force to fear but when it came to thinking their brains lacked any enthusiasm. They attempted to go for something that was too far away and lost everything.

"Mia," Lusark shouted. "I thought you had left."

"No. A bat tried to sell me fruit and instead all I got was a headache," she replied.

"What?" he said confused as ever.

"Never mind, Lusark, you have a race to finish. We'll catch up when we can."

"Great," he replied then turned and stared at Uthuli. Despite his rage for what they had done to his father he too had almost lost his own life and only had Uthuli to thank for being alive. No words were said between the two but a slight nudge of the head to say his thanks. They both understood and expected no less. Time for making up was going to have to come at a later stage. There was a throne to collect and what was perfect was Lusark was getting a crash course on how to be a king on the way.

For the many predators that had competed before in the race for the jungle's throne, each would have a different tale to tell. It was a huge honour even to be lucky enough to enter. Some failed in places where others succeeded but despite this there was always a lesson to be learnt.

Some may have found Crocodile Gorge was the most challenging. Others might have felt that keeping up with the competition was tricky or hunting and keeping fit was a true test of their skill. But one particular part posed a challenge for them all. It was the last stretch of the race where jungle turned to desert. Where the sun had burnt the rivers dry, sucked the life out of all the plants and chased away most of the animals. This was a true test of one's strength and ability to survive. With no shade and no water for miles the desert awaited its prey. Even the eager leopards and hyenas started to slow down in the hope that they could delay the heat of the sun on their backs for even one more second.

They had stopped for one last meal and one last refreshing drink of water. And then pushed on like machines. No longer were they allowed to feel pain or complain about a simple splinter. If they were to survive they were to deny their own impulses.

Lusark had heard of the harsh desert and its hunger to eat all living things, as his grandfather would say. He too prepared himself for the worst. But when he arrived at its gates he was stunned in amazement by what he saw. The change from jungle to desert was as clear as night and day. With sand dunes that piled up as high as the clouds so they formed mountains. It appeared never to end as he could stare as far as the horizon and still only see the empty void of the desert.

"Well, it's now or never," he said to himself and then leaped forward, sprinting faster and faster, hoping that it would somehow end quickly and that if he was lucky he would barely break a sweat.

This was the time the lion would be at its strongest. It was why they had won every other time before. Superior strength and speed would conquer the other predators' lead and would take him to victory. But if his will was not strong the desert would get the best of him. The hyenas certainly had enough will and determination, while the leopards certainly had the experience and knowledge. At that point one would not have known who was to be the victor.

Mia and Uthuli had made their way safely around the gorge and were determined to catch up with Lusark, only something was different with Mia. And Uthuli could see it.

"Mia, what's the matter? Why have you slowed down?" he asked.

"Well, the truth is I haven't eaten in days and I think it's finally starting to wear me out," she replied with very little energy in her voice.

"What? Why have you not eaten?"

"Because I don't hunt other animals and there aren't any berries or fruit around," she explained while slowly starting to tire to her knees.

"Berries? Mia, you are a cat like me, why would you eat berries? We only eat meat. Maybe that was your first problem," he answered in a laughing tone. "And to deny yourself meat because you refuse to hunt, well, that's to deny yourself the right to live."

"I guess food was always served to me from a can. I don't know how I feel about hunting other animals" she replied.

"There is nothing to feel. Maybe one day you'll understand the way of things a little better but for now picture this. We've all been put here for a reason. We all have different needs and ways of fulfilling them. The natural order of your instinct creates the balance in the world. Never deny your instinct." He then moved over to her and passed her some of the meat he had saved. "Here now, you'd better eat or you'll never be able to help your friend."

Mia denied her hunger no longer and dived into the meat Uthuli had given. She seemed to enjoy it despite her previous objections.

"There now, that wasn't so bad was it?" Uthuli asked.

"I guess not, actually it's the best I've ever had," she replied with a touch of guilt in her voice.

"Well, I suggest you eat up. The desert is near and I must warn you that it is not a very friendly place."

Mia couldn't help but worry about her good friend Lusark while she finished her meat. Had he eaten? Was he alright? If only she was with him she would know. The jungle had separated them and put their weaknesses to the test. They had both succeeded so far and had learnt so much about themselves. Maybe a little too fast for the two, who still had a few childish games up their sleeves. But Mia had expected the jungle would have this effect, the day Lusark arrived at her home.

"Wow," she shouted. They had arrived.

"Wow? It's not much to look at but I guess 'wow' is as good a word as any. I hope you are ready for this."

"Wait a second. I have one more suggestion before we go."

"Speak up, girl, I'm all ears," replied Uthuli.

"Well, we're friends now. And every time Lusark and I would run together I would climb on his back to speed things up. So what do you say?"

"I guess that could work," he replied with a smile. "But I should warn you I can run pretty fast. Jump on and let's get out of here."

It was becoming somewhat of a tradition for Mia to ride on the backs of the wildlife's elite, so it only seemed appropriate to add the cheetah to her list. She climbed on and wrapped her paws around him.

"All set," she said.

"We'll see about that," Uthuli laughed.

He started in a mild jog which seemed to have a bit of speed in it but nothing that impressed her. Only the mild pace started to pick up vast amounts of speed in a very short distance. Until finally Uthuli's legs were stretching full length with each tug at the ground. Faster and faster until Mia could barely see what was in front of her.

The wind blew so hard on her face that her lips started to shake all over the place and she was completely unable to show a facial expression. It looked rather uncomfortable but deep inside she loved it. This was the best ride by far but could she hold on long enough?

After hours and hours of running through the desert the others were beginning to feel the pressure. Luckily the day was near its end and they would soon be able to rest in peace. Although 'in peace' involved an empty stomach and a dry, dry mouth.

This was the first night the hyenas decided to get a good night's sleep rather than worry about their usual trickery.

"Well, at least we're still in the lead, my ever graceful leader. I have not seen any of the predators as far as the horizon."

"We're in the desert, you idiot, of course you haven't. It's possible we'll only see them again at the Nile River. That's if they haven't somehow crossed us and taken the lead already."

"Not yet, at least," spoke a voice.

"Ahhh, my furry flying friend. You have returned with good news, I hope. Where is the competition?"

"The leopards have not yet taken the lead but keep close to you," it replied.

"Excellent, so we're still on top then."

"It is not the leopards you must fear in this race. The lion gains on all of you."

"THE LION! What is the lion still doing in the race? You assured me you would misguide them!" shouted Sirus.

"I have separated them but the lion's will is strong. He refuses to give up," replied the bat.

"Well, what good are you then?" asked Sirus.

"Ahh, but very good, for I have a plan of sorts."

"Yes, good old friend. I'm all ears, don't leave me hanging. It's a joke 'cause you like to … Never mind," replied Sirus

"The lion chases after the lead by himself. When you reach the Nile you must join with the leopards and take him out. Tell them they must help finish what was started. And then we can deal with them later. The lion must not make it to the pyramids!" the bat explained.

"Easy, fluff ball. You would swear it was you that was going to be king. Fine, that's what we shall do," replied Sirus. "I must get my sleep so run along, you creep me out just a tinge," he said to the bat as he dozed off.

All was silent in the desert with the leopards, Mia and Uthuli fast asleep. Lusark had never felt so lonely in his life as at that point. With only his thoughts on his mind to keep him company and the light from his old friend the moon, he forced himself to sleep but made a promise to himself that after he had won the throne, he would never let himself be so alone again. Even if Mia had to come to live with him in the jungle after that he would never be short of friends and family again.

Another unforgiving day soon began in the desert. The sun itself rose two extra hours earlier here or so it seemed. And within an instant all were up and all were back in the race.

A bats' eye view watched from the sky where all of the predators could be seen. It was not usual for a bat to come out during the day, but this one had a lot to gain from the winner who was now starting to lose the lead as the others caught up.

The Nile River was going to be the sanctuary for all of them, where food and water would be plentiful and the race was almost at its end. Entering Egypt and being the first to enter the pyramid was a dream vivid in all their minds. It was what got them through their hunger pains and their burning paws, the thought that it would soon be over. But the desert would not release its prey so easily and started to play tricks on all of them.

All began to tire with the constant heat from the sun. And with no water their insides began to dry. The desert had a way of using this against them, by showing things that were not there. Mirages started to pop up everywhere. An oasis called upon their fragile minds, giving them an easy way out that was simply not there.

"Come to me," the desert shouted, "live here in paradise forever. Shade and water and fresh food is but a walk away."

Mia was easily sold and began to venture away from Uthuli. "Mia, where are you going?" he yelled.

"Water, plenty of it just over there," she answered with desperation. She was smaller than the other cats and so her will broke a lot faster.

"It's not real, Mia, just a mirage. Pull yourself together and I will lead you to water."

She couldn't understand how he was not seeing the beautiful

oasis that stood before her. She shook her head to try to snap out of it.

"What? Where is …" It had disappeared right in front of her. "But I could have sworn I had seen trees and a waterhole. How did it …?" Stunned in disbelief, she stood there staring at what was now just dry sand for miles.

"The desert will play tricks on your weaknesses. If you do not deny your impulses she will have you chasing water for days. Come along, little one, we will be fine soon enough."

He was right, for not far from where they were lying was the Nile River, fresh with all that they would need. The leopards had themselves barely arrived at it. They crawled up to the riverbed and drank from the bank.

"Ahhhh, water, my friend, where have you been all my life?" said the leopard king.

But before they could truly enjoy it they were interrupted by the hyenas, who had arrived moments before them.

"Well, well, my brothers, it's been a while hasn't it?" said Sirus.

"Maybe not long enough, Sirus," replied the leopard king. "Why have you shown yourself, unless you want to challenge?"

"Ha, ha, always down to business with you, hey. Well, there is no challenge I wish to have with you. More like a continuation of a previous contract."

"I'm listening, but no tricks," the leopard king replied.

"None, but our little problem with the lions is not over."

"What? How is that possible? We have taken out Kinshasa and his body guard?"

"Yes, but his son is determined to win the royal throne. And I hear he is determined to take us all out. We cannot let that happen. Will you join me one last time and finish what we started, old friend?" asked Sirus.

The leopard king was not as devious as the hyena; in fact it was the hyena's words that convinced him to do what he did the first time. Doing it again was not his intention, but he had come too far to lose it at that point.

"Very well, what is your plan?" said the leopard king.

"Just follow me," replied Sirus.

Unsure whether he had been tricked into following another mirage the desert had made for him, Lusark became rather surprised when he walked right into the Nile.

"WATER!" he screeched. Suddenly he panicked and ran out frantically. He wasn't prepared to go through the same experience he had gone through previously. He approached the riverbed carefully and enjoyed the refreshing cool water of the Nile.

From there he knew that to get to the pyramids he would have to follow it north. A simple task, but how far were the others ahead of him? Determined to catch up, he spent little time in rest.

Along the Nile he bolted, up into the borders of Egypt, where he was met by the people and animals who lived there. They seemed very comfortable with a lion's presence. It seemed Lusark was somewhat of a celebrity as they all started to shout and cheer as he ran through the villages. Clearly the race was known around those parts and if so then they knew who the boss was.

Feeling ever so proud of himself, Lusark found energy that wasn't there before. He ran with all his might, forgetting that arrogance would only harm him, for it had blinded him to the trap that he was running straight into.

The pyramids were in the distance, but he couldn't help but think why he had not seen the others. Had they already finished or had he raced right past them and not even noticed? The goal at hand was so close, he would only let it bother him when he had arrived.

"Help me! Somebody help!" cried a voice.

Lusark ran to the rescue, and found one of the leopards lying down with an injured leg.

"What happened to you?" he asked.

"My king and I were attacked by the hyenas. They broke my paw and took my king with them. Please help me find him."

"Those hyenas have done enough. I will take them out once and for all. You wait here and rest."

He turned around to head for the pyramids where he was sure he would find them. Only to learn that they were right behind him. Worse still, they were with the leopard king and he certainly was in no danger from them. He had been ambushed the same way his father had been. Was he to live the same dark fate of his father?

"Well, well, you silly lion. You should not have come. ATTACK!" shouted Sirus.

Unaware of their poor friend's fate, Mia and Uthuli had reached Egypt, not slowing down for the attention of the villagers.

"We have to find him, I fear something is very wrong," shrieked Mia. She had taken her place on Uthuli's back to speed things up, but were they too late?

ROARRRR! Screams of different cats, but Mia had recognised that one of them had to be Lusark.

"Hurry, Uthuli, hurry," she screamed.

When they found him he was still alive, but the hyenas and the leopards had done their damage. He was covered in his own blood as well as the other predators'. They had ripped him all over and were not looking to stop. He tried to fight them off with his last bit of strength but it was a fast-losing battle.

"LUSARK!" Mia called. "Uthuli, you have to help him."

"It has to stop now!" he replied as he ran off at the pack, roaring with the devil inside him. "ENOUGH!" he shouted.

The others had paused for a second to hear what Uthuli had to say. This was not going to work in the hyenas' favour but keeping quiet was going to avoid them looking guilty of anything.

"Why do you stop us, Uthuli? We thought you were with us," said the leopard king.

"No. I'm not anymore. What we did was wrong, and if winning this means we have to cheat then we don't deserve it. Kinshasa was a fully grown lion but Lusark is barely past being a cub. Do you feel challenged or threatened by him too?"

"The hyenas told us he was coming after us, we were just finishing what we started," the leopard king explained.

"THE HYENAS!" Uthuli replied. "They are betraying us all. They took my brother out at Dead Man's Creek. And now they are using you to take out the competition. They will certainly have the same fate for you."

"Sirus, is this true?" asked the leopard king.

"Well, not really. That was just an accident. My foolish servant may have bumped a rather large boulder over, but it was quite innocent," answered Sirus, who was now starting to fear even his own shadow.

"What?" asked his servant.

"Sirus, if you don't close your mouth right now you're going to be in a lot of trouble with me," shouted Uthuli. "The only reason I'm not doing anything is because I have seen a true king before me and I wish only to act as he does. Lusark has not sought vengeance on any of us, all he wishes to do is finish what his father started. While we could only win by cheating, the true king still stands before all of you. But no longer will you have your way with him."

"Lusark, inside that pyramid are the Siamese cats. I'm sure they are waiting for you. The throne is yours, Sire," he bowed down, facing Lusark.

The leopards joined Uthuli and gave him the rightful respect that not only he deserved, but his father too. The hyenas weren't pleased in bowing but knew they had got off lightly and were in no position to challenge. Mia also bowed to her friend but was stopped.

With little breath Lusark spoke, "No, Mia, you need not bow to me."

She stood up and smiled. "Go, Lusark, your destiny awaits you. I'll be out here when you're done."

He had no energy left in him but still made an attempt to smile back at his friend. "Destiny," he said, and then slowly moved towards the pyramid's entrance. The others had gathered around it, even the villagers and animals that lived there came to see.

He had barely stepped foot inside when he realised that he was about to go through another test. There were many passages that had led into many rooms but there was no direct sign of the Siamese cats. What was now going to be his final battle would not require strength or speed. It was a mental challenge, one that would test his own inner demons.

"Hello, is anyone here?" he said as he passed deeper into the pyramid. But no answer, just more passages that appeared to lead nowhere. He started to fear that if he even tried to turn back at that point he wouldn't be able to find his way out. It was now completely dark. With only his heartbeat echoing against the walls he called out again.

"Hello, I'm looking for the Siamese cats. Are you there?" Before he could continue a voice spoke out, but it sounded as if it was not talking to him but rather about him. It was the elders deciding his future after his father's death.

"He is certainly not strong enough to fill Kinshasa's place. Maybe we should nominate another instead," said the voice.

"I am strong enough. I've made it to the pyramid!" he shouted as he ran from one room to the next, looking for the voice.

"It's never been done before where we would choose another for the throne, it would be an insult to Kinshasa. But sadly we need a leader and Lusark is no leader," continued the voice.

"I am a leader, don't choose anyone else." He became hysterical, lost in the darkness. Feeling useless, he gave in and broke into tears. "I will never be as great as my father," he cried at the voice. "But I'm here and at least I never gave up, so say as you please. No one shall steal the throne from my father's bloodline. NO ONE! Show yourself, coward, and I will show you how much of a leader I am." Enraged, he began to knock at the walls and scratch away into the dark empty space.

"You've made your point, young one," said another voice.

"Who said that? Show yourself," he replied with much rage in him.

"Follow my voice and you shall see." Lusark followed as the voice guided him through the many passages and rooms. "That's it. Keep coming, you're getting closer, Lusark."

Finally he reached a room that had been lit up. It was filled with many ancient Egyptian artefacts. Gold statues and fine silk lay everywhere. In the centre were two small cats that resembled Mia in size, only they looked more alien-like.

"Come closer, young lion," one said. "Congratulations on winning the race."

"I'll come closer but no more games, I've had it," Lusark replied.

"Ahh, but games are so important for us to know if you are fit. Don't worry, the games are over but you must understand that never before has such a young king stood before us. Being a king is not just about being the strongest physically, but he must also have full control over his own inner demons."

"Well, at least have the courage to face them," said the other while scratching the back of its ear.

"The courage to face them! I have nearly died just trying to get here and then you still play on my weaknesses. Have you passed your own test, do you have the same courage to be judged by me? My father died for this quest to become the King of the Jungle. All this has brought amongst the animals that live here is war and deception.

"I do not need your approval or your blessing to be King. I declare this race over." Lusark turned away from the Siamese cats, who didn't seem too shocked at his behaviour.

"Our job is complete," said one.

"Indeed," replied the other.

Lusark found his way out of the pyramid and was met in front by a large number of animals. Mia stood in front. They all took a bow out of respect for their new king.

"All of you stand. None of you should bow to me. For I return not as a king of the jungle but a friend to you all. A friend with no

79

enemies, only brothers of the jungle. So will you accept me not as your king but as your friend?" he asked.

Uthuli stepped out from the crowd and spoke up, "Like you said, a brother."

Suddenly all broke into a cheer of joy as they celebrated their unity with one another. Mia ran up to her friend where she was met with a rather strong hug.

"But, Lusark," she said.

"Yes."

"What about the pride, what will they say?"

"Mia, that is an answer we will only receive when we get there …"

GLOBAL
WARNING

IMAGINE A TIME IN THE world when man and animal were the same. They shared the land equally and everything that it had to offer. From the fruit in the trees to the water in the rivers they lived a life of true respect and equality amongst one another. Man knew which boundaries of the animals they were not to cross and the animals shared the same insight when it came to man.

The world at this time was spiritually connected to all the forms of life that made their home on her vast amounts of land and oceans and had made sure her children never did without.

However, through time man became curious, unsatisfied and bored with life's natural order. This was not man's fault at first as evolution was taking its toll on them, forcing them to develop, forcing them to strive for more creatively, emotionally and spiritually. The animals had not shared this same curiosity man had now developed and so continued their lives as normal.

Over thousands of years man became smarter and more aware of himself and his surroundings. He had been given a gift from the gods, a gift that would give him authority and maturity over all the other creatures that shared the land. With this new understanding the gods had hoped for man to make life good and fair for all and create a sense of purpose.

This sadly was not the case as he was not ready for such a responsibility, he was still too curious of his new-found abilities so that he had lost sight of what was expected of him. The more he learnt the more he wanted to learn, the more he created the more he wanted to create, the more he loved the more he wanted to love. Until a time when he became so obsessed with his own brilliance, that he started to feel less love and less respect and instead more arrogance.

He no longer thought the land was to be shared equally amongst all the creatures. He no longer respected the boundaries of the animals. Anyone who could not think like him did not deserve to eat from the same trees and drink from the same rivers. So with his knowledge he closed up the rivers and removed all the fruit from the trees and stored it for the time when he would want it.

The animals no longer respected man and moved even further away from his presence to try to live in the peace that they knew. Only man's ever growing hunger for food and living space grew faster and faster every passing year. Until there were not many places left for the animals to go.

Man's greed had consumed him to such a point that the gods turned away in shame. Nature herself could not stop them as they were growing too fast. They tore down forests and drank the rivers dry. Finally losing all respect for the world they lived in, they then turned to the animals and began to use them for their own exploitation.

Sadly the oasis that had once given all no longer had anything to give. The world was fast becoming a very unstable place to live. Man's technology was something he himself did not truly understand until it became too late. Tsunamis, floods and melting ice caps were just some of the many things that now posed a threat to every living creature on the planet. Unfortunately this did not stop him from striving on.

Nature had become fed up with man's arrogance. It was time to make things right at any cost ...

In a land far, far away from civilization, ice reigned supreme and life struggled to find its way. This is where the rebellion began, the first-known stand against man and his selfish ways. All the animals of the snow kingdom were summoned by its ruler, General Zukov. General Zukov was an Arctic polar bear whose descendants were the first to offer protection against man to all those who shared the ice regions with them.

They were the first stand against man's destructive behaviour, but had decided to remain neutral unless man had done something wrong first. However, there was never any real threat living in the snow because man never ventured that far. All had been peaceful until now, when Zukov suddenly declared war.

While the large forces of polar bears, wolves and every other snow animal gathered in military quadrants outside the gates of Zukov's ice castle, he waited patiently at his throne for a special delivery. So special he had sent his best flyers, the Atlantic snow owls, to collect it. All was silent inside except for his large nails tapping away at his throne. His second in command and military advisor stood at his side, watching for the moment that the doors would be flung open.

"What is the news of my snow owls? Have they collected her yet? My patience grows thin and my men hunger for the battle. No longer do I wish to hold them off," said Zukov, who seemed rather agitated.

The polar bears believed in two things, equality and never to feel fear. Even though Zukov was a rather large and intimidating bear his men always answered with the same confident tone.

"Your snow owls are but moments away, General. They found her somewhere around the Nile. Supposedly in the middle of some race. Apparently she put up a bit of a fight when they tried to collect her, so they bagged her," replied Vuldez, the General's second in command.

"Well, I hope they did not offend her! She is a very important key in this battle if we are to win!" said the General.

"Those snow owls are highly trained, General, I'm sure once they bagged her the flight was rather comfortable. We had no choice but to apply a little force. As you said we were not to tell her anything until you had spoken to her," explained his military advisor.

Zukov had a lot of animals who were depending on him to make the right decision for them. As he looked out of the window overlooking his army he wondered in fear if he had made the right decision. His mind went to why he started all this in the first place. The thoughts brought so much anger and hatred out of him that he began to rip the throne room apart. The war was certainly going to happen.

High up in the clouds a set of three snow owls flew vigorously through the chilled winds to get to the ice castle. Their sole mission to deliver what was inside the bag they were carrying. A small opening revealed an eye that watched out with anticipation. What was this creature's purpose and how was it going to put the odds in the General's favour?

Suddenly through the thick white clouds of snow an opening led to the castle. Below, the armies of snow creatures could be seen clearly in formation, preparing for something big. With a jilt from their wings they grabbed the air, forcing themselves to stop. The flight seemed over for just a moment as they hovered in the skies, then with a sudden sinking feeling they dove down towards the castle and through a window with synchronized precision.

"Ahhh, my noble warriors of the sky have returned," said Zukov. "And it appears you have delivered as promised."

In-between the General and the owls lay the bag, but there was no movement and no creature to be seen. Then suddenly a head slowly peered out.

"W-w-w-where am I? W-why am I here?" said the creature.

"You are not in harm's way here, little one. I must apologise for the way you have been brought here but time was short," replied the General.

Slowly the creature got out of the bag, looked behind at the owls with a rather nasty stare then turned and took a step forward.

"It's rather small to have such a large reputation, don't you think?" whispered the General to his two advisors.

"Come forward, little one. I am General Zukov, leader of the polar bears and protector of the snow creatures. Can you tell me, are you the one they call the saviour to the kings of the jungles? The one they call Mia?"

"I wouldn't know about 'the saviour' but my name is Mia and my friends are the kings of the jungles," she replied.

"Then, Mia, you are the one we've been looking for. We are faced with a very dark time here on earth. Man has burnt his last bridge with the animal kingdom. They take and they take and they take, when do you ever see them give?" explained the General.

"I'm not sure what you mean, I have seen no such thing," replied Mia. She replied honestly but had never really seen much of man outside of her little village. Her Nana, who she loved, and besides that the occasional postman were all she had to work with.

"Ha, ha, ha," laughed the General. "My poor naïve child, please forgive me. I'm sure a creature as young as yourself knows little of the ways of the world. But with the short time that we have left you must trust me on many issues, for we are in a war that waits for no one."

Trust, Mia knew by now, usually was associated with a knock to the back of her head. She was not too keen on it but still listened to the bear with open ears. After all, if there was a war then she was certainly going to help where she could.

"I understand the urgency, but I have heard of no war," she replied.

"This is a war between man and animal. Every day man eats at the land and destroys it for the animals that live there. If they are not stopped then we shall all face our doom."

The deep concern and fear written on Mia's face spoke for her lack of words. "What ... I ...," she attempted to speak while still trying to make sense of it all. The world seemed fine to her.

"I'm sure this is a lot to take in, Mia, but this is why you must trust me. There is very little time to act. I need you to speak to the lion king of Africa and the tiger king of India. We need them to join forces with us and strike man together at the same time! CATCH THEM OFF GUARD!" demanded Zukov, who was now getting carried away with the idea of a global attack.

If it was so important and there was such a short time, why did her friends of Africa and India not already know? Something didn't seem right with Zukov's eagerness to dive into battle.

"But if I was to do that, get the kings to attack the humans, I mean. What would happen to my Nana and all her friends? She has been so good to me, surely this war is not against all humans?" she asked.

"IT IS WITH ALL THE HUMANS AND THEY WILL ALL PAY FOR WHAT THEY HAVE DONE!" he growled.

This was not a way to convince Mia to help, and the General knew this.

"Forgive me, young one, I am but a poor old bear with a broken heart. Come walk with me, let us talk in private." Mia followed with a sympathetic bone in her body. Or maybe it was just plain curiosity. "This Nana you speak of, she seems very important to you, yes?"

"She is the reason I'm alive today," she replied.

"Then you will understand my pain and my anger. Forgive me if I struggle to tell the story, it happened quite recently."

"My brother, my younger brother, had set out for Greenland. It is customary for every polar bear to prove his manhood, if you will, when he reaches a certain age. It is a tradition we've had for centuries. His safe return deems him worthy of being a polar bear. My seals tell me he had made it and on his way back some of the ice had broken off. He tried to swim to land but it was too far. The seals themselves could not help him as he was too heavy. In the end all they could do was watch as he tired out and began to sink." A tear trickled from the General's eye as he told the story.

"Oh my, I'm so sorry," she said, trying to comfort him.

"That ice has been solid as a rock every century that my family has crossed it. Until recently, when it all just started to melt. Man's technology is the reason for this and this is the reason why they must be eliminated from the history books."

Mia had realised that there was going to be a war, like it or not. But she was still going to try avoiding it if possible.

"Is it fair that all man should pay? They're not all bad, Zukov, there are large amounts of land that I have seen that are untouched by man and his technology, surely there is a way through all this?"

The tears had left Zukov's face and only the anger was left. He started to breathe hard as he stared at her, but was able to keep his calm.

"I knew such a young creature would never have the foresight and leadership it was going to take to see my point. I have already lost my brother but I swear to you I shall not lose another. Man will run, man will fear, and man will disappear from this planet before I am put to rest. And if you are not with me then you are against me, and I suggest you take some time to work out whether that's where you want to be. My forces leave tomorrow at dawn; you have till then to decide." He turned to his wolf bodyguards standing in the distance and ordered them to escort her away. "Send her to a room and make sure she doesn't leave it till I return."

"It would only be a pleasure, my General," replied the wolf.

Mia took a gulp for her breath but struggled to get the air in. There were far too many things to swallow at that moment. The wolves were the icing on top of it as they reminded her of the pesky dogs that would bark at her from the streets in her village.

Wolves were different to dogs though, they didn't seem to have the same clumsy mannerisms. They were focused, on eating perhaps as their teeth always stuck out and they were quite thin in size. This was not good for Mia, who could have been the right-sized portion of a good dinner for one of them. There was something so dark and powerful about them and that was probably why the General had chosen them and not his own bears to guard him.

"This is your room. If you should need anything, anything at all, I'll be right out here waiting. Ha, ha, ha, ha, ha, ha," the wolf sniggered, "sleep well."

Every time Mia had found herself on one of her little adventures the danger was always quite high and she always considered herself lucky to get out alive. But this seemed different altogether, she had no idea where she was and she had no one on her side to help her. Worst of all, she had to make a decision that was going to hurt her either way she chose.

The Nile race had just finished, it was time for her to head home to Nana and not be trapped in a giant ice castle with a crazy polar bear as the host. Sadly she understood what he could have been going through. Maybe he had a point that she just wasn't seeing yet.

"Sleep, Mia, tomorrow will bring the answer," she said to herself as she dozed off.

Never before had she dreaded the idea of the sun rising as she did that night. No simple answer was going to bring the peace, but maybe if she slept the whole thing would just go away. Perhaps this was just a terrible dream that would soon end.

Most nightmares don't end with the ground shaking, but this nightmare had only just begun.

"The General awaits your company. Follow me," said the wolf.

She climbed out of her sleep and moved down the long corridor into the throne room where the General was enjoying his breakfast.

"Ah, Mia, what a pleasant surprise, do come in make yourself at home," General Zukov spoke in a friendly tone, but Mia already knew that his courtesy was as short as his temper. "Are you hungry, do you like tuna?" he asked.

"*Tuna*?" she replied. "If I were the earth tuna would be my sun. Yes, I love tuna. Is it salty, canned or just regular?"

"Regular, I suppose."

He grabbed one from the bowl and dropped it in front of her. This was not the tuna she was used to from the can; this had eyes, a tail and even gills on its sides.

"This is not tuna," she said.

"Correct, it is not just tuna it is the finest tuna you will ever find, freshly caught for me personally. And only my finest and most respected guests have the honour of tasting it," he explained.

She turned to it with big eyes and dove into the first bite. Trying to compliment on how good it was but couldn't stop stuffing her mouth.

"This ... this ... is ... pretty good. Who's your Nana?"

"I'm glad you approve," he answered.

If you were ever to get in Mia's good books food was definitely going to be a winner, not to mention the taste had reminded her of home. Was this just a ploy on the General's behalf or was it genuine generosity? Time would only tell.

"Mia, join me outside. I wish to introduce you to the other animals that have turned to me for help and protection. The ones I call my children and they would call me Nana, if you will. It is important for you to see what depends on you making the right decision."

As they approached the front gates the sheer number of the animals was a frightening experience for her. This is why the ground had been shaking; this was the force that was going to declare war on man.

"Don't be afraid, Mia, come to the front. My fellow animals, this is the one they call Mia, the one who is going to help us win this battle. So we can live in peace once and for all," shouted the General.

"No, wait, I didn't say ..." She was tricked, but could not back out at that very moment. Besides, the roars, screams and cheers of joy were welcomed by Mia's ego. Now before her was the largest and fiercest of armies ever to be seen and they were at her command. The General was right in playing to her ego, for she was now one of them. How could so many animals be so wrong, maybe it was time to do her part? she thought.

"General, I must leave at once and inform the kings of the jungles," she shouted.

"Excellent," replied the General, "I knew eventually you would see it my way. We will wait one more day for you to prepare the jungle animals, and should you need anything my owls will always be near to you."

The snow owls flew down with the carry bag for Mia to be transported and then off they went back towards Africa in search of the kings. Little did she know while she was on her way back in search of Lusark that the lion king was on his way to the Arctic to find her.

He was worried for his friend when the owls came down and dragged her off, and so spent no time resting. It was not hard to trace the snow owls' footprints as they only worked for the general of the polar bears. He knew he was getting closer as the weather got colder. But his anger and determination to get Mia back kept him warm.

As the afternoon sun rose over the ice castle the General found peace at his throne. He had achieved a lot in the day just by getting Mia to join forces with him. Things were looking up for him but not for too much longer. As he sat deep in thought the shouts of his name could be heard from the corridors.

"General, General," cried one of the wolf scouts as he barged into the throne room.

"You'd better have a good reason for disturbing my peace in such a vile manner," Zukov replied.

The wolf tried to catch his breath before speaking again. "A lion heads for the castle. The lion king heads for the castle! Perhaps he is looking for his friend. Perhaps he is upset for the way we took her away."

"Oh, grow a spine, if he is on his way then that is perfect. We can talk about the war and if he doesn't like the idea we will capture him and use him as a bargaining tool. Let him pass through," said Zukov.

"Yes, General, I will assemble some of my men to wait in the shadows."

At this point Lusark had reached the gate but was not welcomed with a pleasant introduction. He couldn't help but wonder why the armies were assembling and why he was being allowed to walk right into the castle. His instinct told him they were expecting him. But that could have been good or bad.

Down the long corridor he could hear paws sneaking behind him and short silent breaths puffing away in the darkness. He had no choice but to walk on if he wanted to find his friend. Finally he reached the throne room.

"Ah, Lusark, welcome, welcome. I am General Zukov. I knew your father when you were just a little …"

"Enough with the games. I am not here to have small talk. Where is Mia and why have you taken her?" interrupted Lusark.

"Ha, ha, of course, my friend, sit down and relax and all will be told to you. There is a great war between man and animal. They pollute our waters and kill our loved ones every day and it is now time we strike back. Man doesn't care for us and he is forcing us to extinction."

"Where does dragging Mia off into the sky involve this war?" answered Lusark.

"She has many powerful friends such as yourself, I only wished to ask her for her help to unite us all."

"Then where is she? Let me see her."

"Not possible. She has left to go to speak to you and get you involved," said Zukov.

"Mia would never agree to such a thing, and why do none of the jungle animals know of this war against man? Why would we just take them all out?" argued Lusark.

"Ah, my poor young naïve boy, I knew you would not understand such a thing at such an age. THAT IS WHY I MUST DO THIS FOR THE GOOD OF YOUR KIND TOO! Wolves, take him away."

Sharp, piercing teeth suddenly surrounded Lusark on all sides. He had no choice but to surrender. But before they took him to the dungeon the wolf leader thought it would be good practice for his men to attack the king of the lions. Poor Lusark was getting used to being attacked by groups of predators but the pain never changed. When they were finished with him they dragged him away and locked him up.

"I'm sorry to do this, and one day I'm confident that you'll know why I did. But I can't have anyone second-guessing my men when we go into battle," said the General.

"Well, you'll never get the jungle animals to agree to this, Zukov."

"Oh, but that battle has already been won. If they don't fight for me I will kill their king. Now if you'll excuse me, I have a war to plan. Your father would have fought by my side, I guess you aren't lion enough to do the same."

With the lion king locked away Zukov no longer had to wait for Mia to get the message through. Still, she was a bargaining tool for the tiger king of India and he was not going to let that go. If kidnapping was going to get him his army he was prepared to go all the way.

"Send word to the owls; tell them to return home immediately. I have other plans for Mia," commanded Zukov. "Tomorrow at dawn we leave for the cities of man."

"General, I would advise we made some plan with the jungle animals before we do that," advised Vuldez.

"That is why you are second in command, Vuldez, I have already sent allies to the jungles. And I'm quite sure they will join us when they hear what I have to offer them in return. Ha, ha, ha."

Although it seemed all of General Zukov's plans were coming together this was not truly the case. Ironically the more his plans came together the more he was starting to come apart. His mind was no longer thinking sensibly and filled with the rage in his heart, his motives were no longer clear.

He was once a loving bear who lived his life in peace with his family. He had lost a brother, but was he going to now lose himself? His plans to attack were not well thought out, and when he believed he was doing it for the good of all animals he was making more enemies than friends. He had avoided his pain in the hope that after the war it would be easier to bear. But this would never be true.

Another irony was the word 'ally' in this story, for the allies that he had sent were more devious creatures than man himself. The ones who could not live with man or animal, for none could trust them, now had become the messengers of war.

Through the thick, moist plantation of the Indian jungle the black panther roamed in search of the tigers. His dark complexion shadowed him in even the lightest parts of the land. This suited his personality as he always liked to watch secretively. He travelled by himself, unafraid for he knew of something important to the tigers, something that would make them go to war.

As they sat in peace, bathing themselves and preparing for their afternoon nap, the King became aware of the panther's presence.

"How long are you planning on sitting in those bushes, watching us?" asked the tiger king. "I can sense that you are unafraid so why do you continue to hide from us?"

"I guess old habits die hard," said the panther as he revealed himself. "I am Shadick."

"Yes, Shadick, why have you come to see us?" asked the tiger king, who felt no need to continue the formal greeting. He knew that the panther had no good news to bear.

"I have come on behalf of General Zukov, the leader of the polar bears. A war begins between man and animal and he has requested you join his forces here in India."

"I do not know a General Zukov and I certainly won't fight without purpose. Tell your General I deny the invitation," replied the tiger king.

The panther was enjoying the moment, for next was going to be a threat and that was something he lived for.

"You may not know the General but he assured me that you would know a small village cat named Mia," said Shadick.

"What! Mia! What about her!"

"Oh, nothing yet, but at dawn tomorrow if you do not attack the cities she will be something of a memory, if you catch my drift."

Suddenly the King's guards surrounded Shadick, who could now only hiss in fear of his opponents. Threatening the King was punishable by death. However, Mia was the one who had helped them find their rightful place back at the throne. They had to think smart if they wanted to ensure her safety.

"Be careful, my friends, if she means anything to you I would obey like good little pussy cats. The war has begun and you will have your part in it. Tomorrow you will attack the cities, you and all the animals of the jungle. I'll be there to make sure your loyalty is sufficient."

As the tiger king cursed the complicated situation he was forced into, the lions too had been dealt with their burden. The hyenas had their part in delivering the message from Zukov. They could not choose their king over any other, yet fighting with no purpose seemed a true challenge of their morality. As the day came to an end the jungle animals had agreed on declaring war for their loved ones. Hoping some divine power would intervene.

Zukov had his army and the war was set to go. With just a night separating peace from chaos many animals struggled to sleep. The world was going to be a new place in the morning. On the one side, things stood a great chance of improving for the animals. Man was no saint and only the animals' silence allowed the abuse to continue. This could have been their chance to earn the respect that they so deeply deserved.

On the other side, things had a chance to get much worse. How far would a war have to go and would man be prepared to change his selfish ways? Despite the fact that Zukov was making enemies in every possible way maybe someone like himself was required to make a difference. One couldn't help but think what the outcome was going to be ...

"General, the owls have arrived back with Mia. What shall we do with her?" said the wolf.

"Bring her to me, I'm sure she has questions to ask and I would love to answer them," he replied.

The wolves obeyed the order and brought her in, but she was not pleased with her treatment.

"Why did the owls not take me to Lusark, why have you brought me back?" she asked.

"Ah, Mia, always a pleasant surprise to see you. Let me be as straightforward as possible. I have Lusark locked away in one of my dungeons for his disobedience. Bad pussy cats get no milk before bed. However, you might still have an opportunity to get yours. Get him to agree to fight in this war and we will not harm him any further," said the General.

"What do you mean any further! What have you done to him?"

"Oh, Mia, bless your fighting spirit. But save your energy for where it is needed. Now either you convince him or you sleep in the dungeons as well."

"OK, General, you've made your point, I will do what you ask if you keep your promise."

"Agreed," he answered.

Mia had come too far in her journeys to be bullied by some bear, it was time she used trust to her own advantage.

The General took her down to the dungeons to meet with Lusark, but when she got there Lusark was in the same bad shape as when she had last seen him after the Nile race. Still, they were both pleased to see one another.

"Alright, enough with the touching moment. Get down to business, you have five minutes," demanded the General.

"Yes, General," she replied as he shut the door. "Lusark, I don't know what we're going to do but if you don't agree to fight he will harm you. Play along until we can figure out the next step," she continued.

"Mia, you had gone to find me so you could convince me of this very thing. And now here you are," said Lusark.

"I don't really know what I was thinking at the time, I guess I got caught up in the moment. But I know it's wrong and the only way we can help is if we aren't locked up. Just follow my lead in the morning …"

"Alright, time's up. What is your decision, lion?" asked the General.

"If my friend here thinks it's a good idea then so do I, I will fight with you," replied Lusark.

"Good, now I hope you don't take it personally but you will sleep here tonight. I would hate to find you gone in the morning. As for you, Mia, join me for some milk and tuna upstairs as a reward for your good work. Sleep tight, Lion King."

Both Mia and the lion king played along to the General's tune in the hope that his trust could later be used against him. Until then they could only smile and agree.

In the cities man followed a daily routine which usually started around 7 a.m. They would wake up, clean themselves and then after a quick breakfast they would jump into their modes of transport and hurry along to work. In a modern world, in a modern society, time controlled all. Like the machines they built, they too had become small moving parts in a larger mechanical workforce.

Blind to their own existence, they consumed and created oblivious to its effects. In the city the early bird always caught the worm, or in this case the fish as the fisherman cast their boats off for the morning catch. Little did they know what was waiting for them. As their boats came to rest a few miles out from the harbour, the rapid waters were fast becoming a concern for them.

"Hey, Joe, check the weather for any storms on the way. The water should never be this rough out here," said the fisherman.

Joe was about to take a chunk out of his breakfast when the water suddenly sucked in and blew out again. "Whales? It's not possible, not this close to the harbour," yelled a very frightened Joe.

Oh, but it was a whale swimming right up under the boat and with a high-pitched cry the war had begun. Out of the water, up into the air it rose, colliding on top of the boats, smashing them into splinters. The fishermen swam for their lives towards the harbour but soon realised that that was not the place they should have been heading for.

Whale after whale started to surface, pushing the smaller boats under and rocking the bigger ones to the point of tilting over. The coastlines were being attacked from all sides. Dolphins and sharks worked together in other regions, forcing anyone who wanted to take a morning swim to flee for their lives. All hell had broken loose and man wasn't sure what to think of it.

While the city remained distracted with the ocean, General Zukov led his large armies across the glaciers. Mia and Lusark stood close to his side, looking for some way to stop the war from happening. Lower down in India and Africa the lions and tigers along with all the jungle animals now reached the borders of the cities. So far there was nothing to stop them. From the north to the south and the east to the west the continents' cities became surrounded by bird, mammal and fish.

On an average day for man he would see cars, buildings and an occasional hot dog stand outside his place of business. Wildlife was something they enjoyed if they went to the zoo on weekends but today was special for all of them. Today they were getting a front row seat of the nature channel.

When the General and his army finally reached the city borders Mia tried to convince Zukov to call off the war before it got ugly and went too far. Only, his ego was not going to allow for it, especially with the taste of vengeance so near.

"Zukov, please stop this madness. There has to be another way to make things right," she requested.

"Ah, I should have known that you and this lion would have tried to stop me somehow. It's too late for that, now we fight. Guards, take these two to the back and do not let them go. History is being written and you shall see it all," he replied.

As Lusark and Mia were dragged to the back things started to slow down for poor Mia. She couldn't help but think what was going to happen to Nana through all this. Everything was so intense and loud. The animals' once-peaceful natures had now been poisoned with hatred and anger. Like Zukov said, it was too late to turn back, things had already gone too far.

Birds flew by the hundreds above the buildings while thousands upon thousands of animals eagerly waited to storm down the gates of man. Some of the animals had not shared the same views on the attack but all were still there and all were going to fight. And with the words 'Animals, take back your land!' the war of man and animal had begun.

The animals stormed into the cities, causing chaos everywhere. Man, woman and child had no time to even defend themselves; all they could do was run for their lives. Fleeing everything they owned and everything they knew as their lives. Many tried to hide but were soon found by the keen sense of smell that the animals possessed.

Although the animals seemed hostile it appeared that General Zukov had no intention of harming anyone. Except maybe for the occasional man who would try putting up a fight. He wanted man to respect him and fear him while breaking down a little bit of the human dignity.

Mia and Lusark watched from the outskirts of the city where man now started to flee. The General had chased them out of their homes and out of the cities, forcing them now to live with nature. Mia hoped that Nana would be fine if they did the same in her village.

"Lusark, I need to find my Nana and make sure she is alright, before I do anything else."

"And I need to find my pride and let them know I'm safe so they can stop fighting. I will find you, my friend, and then we shall make things right," he replied.

Luckily the guards that were keeping an eye on them got caught up in the war and left them free to run off.

"That's it, Man, no longer will you have your technology, run along before I change my mind." At this point Zukov had noticed the guards he had ordered to hold Mia and Lusark were standing near to him. "What are you doing here, you fools! Where are those cats?" They could only look at him with blank confusion. "Never mind them, there's nothing they can do now. I have a new mission for you, find me the biggest, most luxurious building this city has to offer and set up post. It will be my new castle where I shall rein supreme."

"Yes, my General," replied the wolf as his pack raced off into the city in search of the finest building there was.

So at the end of that day Zukov was cheered on by the animals all over the world. He had led them to victory and a new possibility of peace. A peace that they knew and respected and now man was faced with surviving in the wild.

It was many sunsets later that Mia still found herself heading towards her village in search of Nana and her three sisters. She had lost weight and looked dirty to the bone. After all, her journeys home were always with Nana and if she could no longer find that, she no longer knew where she was. Nana had become a compass in her world of adventure.

This thought of losing Nana left her caring very little for food or cleanliness and more concerned about getting home. While she travelled through the African wastelands she wondered if Lusark had found his pride and would she ever see him again.

Africa had never looked so plain and dry before but perhaps that was because all the animals were no longer there. They had moved into the cities and found new homes and nesting grounds, feeding off the leftovers of food and water man had left. Zukov thought he had made things better but this was not the world intended for the animals, things were very wrong and the natural order of things was now upside down.

Just before another night had ended Mia had reached her little village, which now looked as dirty and desperate as she. She made her way down the little road that had led her to her first journey into Africa. But the excitement that it once gave her now could only take back what it had given. A different noise now buzzed from the village, which was filled with howls of hyenas, jackals and wild dogs.

The gate that closed her into the garden she played in now lay open for anyone to come and go as they pleased. This was not a good sign for her. She took a big breath and then climbed in through the window. The house was dark and quiet with things moved all over the place. Her home had lost its gentle touch that once flourished from Nana's presence.

As she walked into the bedroom she made a silent cry for anyone that was there, Meow.

No reply left her short on hope. Where could they be? she thought to herself. As she walked out a cupboard door opened with a squeak.

"Mia? Mia, is that you?"

It was poor old Nana, she had been hiding away from the animals. Despite that Mia couldn't speak to her she showed her appreciation with a bigger cry.

"MEOW!"

After that her sisters came climbing out of the cupboard, excited to see her.

"Oh, Mia, I thought I would never see you again. All these animals are being so naughty, we had to hide away. I wasn't sure where you were after you ran away with that lion," said Nana.

All Mia could do was look up at her and cry out, "Meow, meow."

"Why are your friends from the jungle acting so silly? Why would they want to stay in a house when they had an entire jungle to play in? Well, either way we are staying put in this house until they come to their senses."

Nana was right. The animals were being silly, why would they want to live in a house when they have an entire jungle? If only someone could point that out for them. Mia decided she was going to stay with Nana and leave the heroism up to someone else for a change. She was going to stay right at home where she belonged.

'Where she belonged' – such a simple term for one who was living it. But this was no longer a reality for man and animal. All was very wrong and was not going to change anytime soon. As the days went by, Mia, Nana and her three sisters, Bella, Coco and Linky, ate through the leftover food in the kitchen until there was not much left. Too afraid to leave the house, Nana was unable to stock up with the food they needed to survive. Mia, out of one last desperate attempt, decided it was time to use a few hunting skills to provide for her family. As Nana and the girls sat starving in a dark corner of the bedroom Mia entered and dropped a small piece of meat on the floor in front of them. They all went into shock.

"What's the matter, girls? I know it's raw meat, but when times are hard you just have to dig in." She tried to encourage their spirits but they remained in shock.

Suddenly a thumping sound came behind her, she turned around slowly. But there was no reason to fear. Her good friend Lusark had come to find her and he too had brought a meaty snack in case anyone was hungry. But unfortunately the sheer size of him, and also perhaps the blood dripping from his face, kept Nana and the sisters in shock despite that he was a friend of Mia's.

"I think we should go and talk outside, lions might be a bit of a big step for the girls after all the chaos," said Mia.

"OK, no problem," replied Lusark.

They moved on down into the garden where they sat under the tree.

"Did you find the pride, Lusark? Is everyone OK?" she asked.

"All is well but I'm concerned for the humans, they cannot survive out in the jungle. And worse, the animals cannot survive in cities. We need to do something to make the peace," replied Lusark.

"You are right, Lusark, but I can't leave my Nana and sisters here again with the hyenas running around. I could never stand to lose them."

Suddenly Lusark became distracted. "Shhhhh, we have a little spy on our hands," he whispered.

It was one of the General's snow owls, but was it there to spy or for some other curious reason? The General had already won the war, so why was it there?

"Wait, Lusark, something is wrong. The General has no other use for us," she said.

"I don't know about that, Mia, he can't be trusted."

The owl continued to stare at them and then revealed the carry bag that Mia had become so familiar with.

"The General wants to see me for some reason," she said.

"No, Mia, he is the enemy."

"That is true, but if I don't go we'll never have a chance to fix things. Stay here and take care of Nana till I get back."

Mia climbed into the owl's bag and was carried away to General Zukov's new castle in the city while Lusark stayed outside the house and guarded Nana and her sisters. What the General wanted with her plagued her mind on the way but something else was beginning to cross her thoughts.

Why now for the first time was the owl struggling to carry her in the bag? It seemed weaker, even its pure white complexion had faded for some reason. All these questions would soon be answered.

Flying over the cities, she could see first hand what effects the animals had on them. As power supplies and generators faded the city buildings started to cast shadows over the streets. While animals raided cars and empty buildings the moon watched with a tearful eye. This did not seem like a promising future.

In the near distance was a building so tall it could have touched the clouds. Mia knew this would have suited the General's ego. Once again through a window they shot up and down corridors until they reached a type of large conference hall. Seated in the centre of course was the General, but no longer with his two advisors at his side. He seemed distant and worn down.

"General, why have you requested me?" she asked but there was no reply. "General, could I have an answer?"

He looked up at her and smiled in a very displeased manner as he got up and walked to a table filled with all types of sweets and junk food. Obviously not the usual diet the General was used to, it appeared he had grown a bit of a sweet tooth.

"Hello, Mia," he replied with a hiccup and a giggle. "It is so very good to see you again. As you can see, I'm doing very well. In case you didn't hear, the animals have won the war, the humans have fled to the jungles and I have a bigger castle."

She knew the General wasn't the most straightforward thinking of creatures but this was just ridiculous.

"Yes, General, I do know this. You have got exactly what you wanted."

"Then why am I so miserable! I feel unfulfilled, do you know that I haven't looked out of those windows in days. I don't even speak to my second in command anymore. Is he still alive? I couldn't even tell you. What is this, Mia, why do I feel like this?" he asked.

"Well, General, maybe it's because you are living in the city of man where you don't belong," she answered rather sarcastically.

"It's exactly what I thought; they've put some kind of voodoo spell on me to make me feel like this. Some kind of last attack to win back the city, try to break the General down, hey. That's it, we are going back to war, and tomorrow we head for the jungles where we will take out man." Clearly the General was starting to lose the plot, but this was not an uncommon thing to happen after a war.

"General, man has not done anything to you. Like you said yourself, you have won the war and chased man from the cities. I think you feel down because you don't belong here and neither do the rest of the animals, eating junk food and candy-coated fudge. You're a bear, you like tuna fish and the ice-cold waters."

What she was saying made sense to him, but after all he had gone through to get there and make his point, would it have all been in vain?

"You are right. I do miss my home and even though this is bigger, who cares? I miss my ice castle. But if I tell the animals to leave man will just go back to his old ways and I can't have that, we can't have that," he replied.

"I think you've already made your point to man and now it's time for you to make the peace and leave it to the chance of fate."

The words she spoke seemed to paralyze him momentarily, and then he spoke just three simple words, "Mia, go home."

She said nothing in reply and knew that if anything was going to work she was going to have to take a bit of her own advice and leave it to fate and hope that enough had been said to make a difference. One more time she was carried off into the skies by the snow owls. While they flew home a strange sense of comfort overcame her. She wondered if that was going to be the last time she would see her little flying friends.

When she finally arrived home she was pleased to see her good pal Lusark sleeping outside the front door of Nana's house. Guarding almost like a really large watchdog. She climbed up her favourite tree quietly so as not to wake him and watched the sun rise in peace.

Not to her surprise, she noticed the jungle animals as they moved down the little road. At this point Lusark had woken.

"The animals, where are they all going?" he asked as he climbed up into the tree with her.

She replied with a rather pleased and confident tone, "Oh, they're going home where they belong."

Lusark looked at Mia in amazement. "I don't know how you do it, Mia, but you do."

She smiled as she lay back against the tree and continued to watch the sun.

"Well, I guess I've got to go back to being king of the jungle. Stop by for dinner anytime," he said.

"Will do ...," she replied before falling into a deep sleep. Lusark jumped over the wall and headed back to the jungle where he was needed. Man was confused by the animals' strange behaviour but realised that they no longer wanted to fight. They too began moving back to their homes. Something was different that day, the queues of animals and man walked side by side. For the first time in a long time they were equal.

General Zukov led his snow creatures back to the ice castle where he learned to find the peace inside himself again. Strangely it was something he could only receive after he had given it. Man and animal respected one another from then on, and to show his willingness for peace, every year Zukov would leave his castle and run out to the borders of the cities and give a giant roar. Man welcomed it every year with cheers of joy and love.

Imagine a time in the world when man and animal were the same. They shared the land equally and everything that it had to offer. From the fruit in the trees to the water in the rivers, they lived a life of true respect and equality amongst one another. A time when man used his knowledge to make a better world for all.

This was the world that Mia came to call home ...

The End